Ghost Stirs the Pot

A COZY GENIE AND ADRIANA DARLING MYSTERY

Carmen Radtke

Contents

1. Chapter 1 — 1
2. Chapter 2 — 12
3. Chapter 3 — 21
4. Chapter 4 — 31
5. Chapter 5 — 43
6. Chapter 6 — 49
7. Chapter 7 — 56
8. Chapter 8 — 68
9. Chapter 9 — 79
10. Chapter 10 — 88
11. Chapter 11 — 97
12. Chapter 12 — 100
13. Chapter 13 — 107
14. Chapter 14 — 116

15. Chapter 15   129

16. Chapter 16   134

17. Chapter 17   143

18. Chapter 18   152

19. Chapter 19   160

20. Chapter 20   169

21. Chapter 21   176

22. Chapter 22   183

23. Chapter 23   191

24. Chapter 24   197

About the Author   204

Also By   206

Cast of characters   208

Chapter One

"Be careful." Primrose Schuyler wrung her hands.

"I promise." I steered her towards her sister Dahlia, who cried into her handkerchief. "Please, go inside, before you catch a cold."

They both dithered.

"I can't concentrate on rescuing Petey if I'm distracted because I worry about you two."

Primrose took her sister by the hand. "Genie's right, my dear. We've got to have faith."

I waited until the two seventy-something ladies closed the door behind them. "The coast is clear," I said. "You can now work your magic."

"The poor sweetheart." Adriana floated onto a branch high up on the oak tree where parrot Petey hid.

The bird was the apple of Primrose and Dahlia's eye. He was also in shock. An hour ago, a window left open by a cleaner had been too much for him to resist. Unfortunately, Petey's newfound taste of freedom came with a lot of dangers, real and imagined. He'd been fine until a red kite soared above him, and on the ground, a cat meowed. Now Petey was too scared to move a muscle or a feather.

I knew all this because Adriana told me. It would take all her powers of persuasion to guide the parrot down and inside, where he belonged.

I wished I could give her a hand, but my climbing skills were not up to that task. Also, whereas the bird trusted Adriana implicitly, I might startle him. After all, I'm just a human he's seen a couple of times.

Adriana on the other hand is a pet-whisperer extra-ordinaire. She's also my great-great-aunt - and a ghost. Officially she died in 1929, at the age of 21. In reality, she materialized in the same villa she took her first and her last breath in, a few months ago, and has been sharing my life ever since.

Up in the tree, she made coaxing sounds at the back of her throat.

Petey hopped to a lower branch. He moved his head back and forth.

Adriana continued to encourage him, until finally, ghost and bird both came down. "Now hop onto Genie's shoulder," she told the bird.

He obeyed, careful to hold on to me without digging his claws in too deep.

Together, we stood outside the door. I knocked. "I've got him."

Primrose opened, and with a last look at my great-great-aunt, Petey flew inside, back to the safety of his aviary.

"You saved him. I don't know what we would have done without you, Genie." Primrose's voice shook.

"I'm glad I could help."

Adriana glowed with pride. She waved the parrot a cheerful goodbye before we dashed home.

The rescue mission meant that I needed to hurry. It also meant that my great-great-aunt could chalk up another good deed on her growing list of successful rescue missions. Adriana Darling was on the way to becoming the unrecognized good spirit of Cobblewood Cove.

Our orange tabby Cleo interrupted her preoccupation with tufting a rug and shedding all over the apartment, to come and greet Adriana.

I received a quick meow, to acknowledge that I, too, had been noticed. I took my overnight bag from the storage cupboard, ready to be packed later.

Cat and ghost froze and glared at me.

"It's only for one night." I snatched my keys. If I didn't make it downstairs fast, I'd be late for work, and I was never late. It was one of my proudest traits, the fact that people could rely on my word.

"Are you at least going to explain the situation to Matt this time?" Adriana pulled herself up to her full height. Her slender frame vibrated with annoyance. Her voice could have cut glass, in a rare change from the dulcet tones she used for any mention of my boyfriend.

It would have been more impressive if I hadn't seen the exact pose and expression only the night before, although in that instance the furious blonde had been 1930s movie star Madeleine Carroll and not Adriana Darling.

I took a step towards the door.

She spread her arms across the frame. "You have to tell him."

Cleo, who invariably sided with my great-great-aunt, took an empty swipe at me, which for this little cat was the equivalent of counting down to three strikes.

At least that's what I'd been told by a trustworthy source.

Said source switched tactics. Her shoulders slumped, and a deep sigh escaped her. "You can't imagine how much it hurts to be left out in the cold."

Hah. "I'll turn on the heating."

"Genie? Who are you talking to?" A voice rang out on the landing. Jilly Pepper, my friend and sometime business partner had come to help me with my merchandise.

Adriana stomped her foot. In tense moments like this, she preferred my undivided attention.

"Nobody," I answered Jilly.

I motioned Adriana to move aside.

She remained stuck to the spot.

I closed my eyes and took a big stride towards her, my hand stretched out. For a second, I felt a tingling sensation as my fingers merged with her body. Then she stepped aside.

She didn't really need to do that. After all, I was the only human in the world who could see my beautiful relative in all her splendor, from her wavy blonde hair and silk evening dress down to her spangled shoes.

I wasn't sure if she appeared to animals or if they only sensed her. Whatever was the case, they found her irresistible. Cleo was the best example.

"I'll talk to you later," I whispered before I joined Jilly. At least I had a few hours to think about my course of action. Now I was the one sighing.

Jilly had already run ahead of me, down the wooden staircase. Her heels clicked on the polished floorboards which dated back to Adriana's days. Like my dear relative, I'd come close to breathing my last here as well, but Adriana had saved me when we had to play a dangerous game to unmask a murderer.

A surge of happiness washed over me. My life had never been as crazy or complicated before I met my great-great-aunt, but it also had never been exciting.

I breezed past my mother's apartment on the first floor, which currently sat empty for a couple more nights. She and her new husband used the villa she'd inherited as a second home, which meant that most weeks, I had the free run of it.

Well, Adriana and I had the free run of it.

For a few weeks, Jilly had occupied the guest suite, until she'd moved in with her boyfriend Kenji, an up-and-coming architect. They'd met when she first came to Cobblewood Cove after we'd lost the lease of our shared city apartment plus studio at the very edge of New York, where *Darling Designs* and *Pepper's Pots* created handmade jewelry and ceramics for the discerning few.

Jilly had since picked up new customers in the tea rooms, cafés, and B & Bs in the area, and I had branched out into a second business venture.

That's what she had come to help me with this morning. Together, we lugged six heavy containers of ice cream into her station wagon. *Gem and Gelato* had already found a loyal clientele in town since Adriana and I'd returned from Italy.

Taking a gelato-making class there at the end of a treasure hunt of sorts with Adriana had been the best decision I could have made. It supplied me with the steady income my bespoke jewelry had thus failed to achieve, and it gave Adriana a sense of accomplishment.

I did the mixing, churning, and selling.

My spectral relative decided which secret ingredient would turn our ice cream from a mouthwatering treat to unbeatable delight. Dead or not, her nose and tastebuds were unrivaled.

The only person who came close to her talent was Pierre, the owner of the oldest delicatessen and diner in Cobblewood Cove. Generations of his family had stood at the ovens in the white clapboard building. The recipes of *Butler's Pantry* were a well-kept secret and had been handed down from son to son or daughter since the first Pierre. He'd been a Huguenot immigrant called Bouteillier, who set foot on this soil not long after the town had been founded over two centuries ago. The last name had been anglicized to Butler, but the moniker Pierre stuck and, like the recipes, was passed down through the generations.

Whatever the Butlers cooked up transported customers to culinary heaven. The family had catered for early movie stars and darlings of the theater as well as for politicians, socialites, and, according to rumor, once for "King Solomon", the uncrowned leader of the Boston underworld during Adriana's lifetime.

That little bit of information I had from her. The rest was common knowledge.

Pierre and I had always been on friendly terms, despite the fact that he was 40 years my senior and I'd only sporadically spent time with my parents in Cobblewood Cove.

Both my mom and dad had set their sights on bigger things than a small coastal town that took its name from a cove no larger than two baseball fields. For me, Cobblewood Cove had been heaven with the sandy beach, the ocean, and the old movie theater, where a uniformed usherette would bring ice cream sodas and milk duds to the seats.

Childless Pierre had been a mainstay of my vacations, and once he'd discovered that I preferred his cooking to every other diner or clam chowder shack around, he'd become almost like an uncle to me.

He'd been the one who inspired me to start a now mostly defunct food blog in my student days, and he'd also been the one who supported my new business.

"Stop daydreaming," Jilly admonished me. She almost disappeared behind the two large stainless steel containers with today's gelato in her arms. Only her curly topknot which she'd lately dyed pink, and her butterfly sunshades were easily visible.

I carried in the rest while Jilly brought in her latest wares. She'd made platters and bowls for Pierre and me, which our customers could also purchase.

Gem and Gelato was located in one corner of the long room that made up *Butler's Pantry*, where three tables sat ready for a small lunch crowd. The walls were covered with old photographs, showing the family members, staff, and customers throughout the years, all the way back to the 1870s. The names written underneath were proof of the familial feeling. There were Butlers and Wards, Schuylers, Darlings, and a couple of almost exotic names like Johansson and Koslowski.

Usually, Pierre would give me a quick wave to greet me as soon as I set foot in the door. Today, he ignored me, and so did the blonde woman who was arguing with him.

I'd seen her around on a few occasions, but up to now, she'd been mild-mannered. It took me a little to remember her name. Katie something, that's all I came up with.

She had her back turned to me, but I saw her shake her fist in Pierre's stony face.

"You're a liar, and I won't be standing for this," Katie snarled before she turned on her heel and stomped off.

"Careful," Jilly said as the woman, who towered over Jilly's five foot two, brushed past her.

Pierre waggled his eyebrows at us. "Sorry."

"No worries," Jilly said. She snapped on surgical gloves and ran her fingers over every bowl and every platter before she declared herself satisfied.

I gave her a gentle nudge. "Off with you and don't forget to have fun."

"Says the woman who hides herself away in that old villa."

I shrugged. As much as I loved Jilly, who could be counted upon to be as easily excited about a thing as she could be distracted, I had no intention of telling her about Adriana.

Believing in chakras and karma and the power of numbers and the right shade of lipstick was one thing. Being told the sanest, most balanced person she knew, aka me, shared her life with a vivacious ghost might be a step too far. Plus, even if she believed me, I couldn't expect Jilly to keep a secret of this magnitude from Kenji. Or, after a few beers, from my mother.

"Try to sell out my stuff while I'm gone," she said. "If it works, I could branch out further afield."

"I'll try." I held the door open for her. "See you in a week."

She blew me a kiss and headed for her car, to set off for a week's vacation at Niagara Falls.

I found Pierre helping himself to samples of my gelato.

"This is your best batch yet," he declared.

I frowned. Something was wrong. Pierre always waited for me to offer him a taste.

At the age of 72, his habits were firmly ingrained, down to the number of times he wiped each shoe on the mat before entering the deli when he'd gone outside for his daily walk to the square and back. He caught my concerned glance. "Forget the woman. She was just complaining about something that didn't happen," he said with an air of finality.

That would explain it. Like me, Pierre reached for sweet things when the going got tough.

In the kitchen at the back pots and pans clanged and meat sizzled.

My mouth watered.

Pierre's second in command, Steve Hiller, did most of the work these days. Only the final touches, when the real magic happened, were still reserved for Pierre. He and he alone would be in the kitchen to add whatever secret ingredients made the dishes irresistible. In the meantime, Steve would either meet his fiancée at one of the tables or when she was busy, he'd sneak out for a quick browse at *Nuts and Bolts*, the local hardware store.

Steve spent half his paycheck there, while he was restoring an old farmhouse and brewery just outside the city limits.

Pierre put his gelato bowl and spoon on a trolley.

For takeaways, we used paper cups, bamboo cutlery, and cardboard boxes. For everything else, Pierre insisted on bone china, ceramic plates, and real silverware.

Customers who brought their own mug for a coffee to go earned a discount. We took our environmental responsibility seriously. He also insisted that plastic affected the perception of taste and not in a good way.

Pierre smoothed back his silvery hair that still held traces of black, dithering as if deciding if he should say anything else to me before kitchen duty called.

While he was still making up his mind, the front door was pushed open so abruptly that I gave a start. Pierre muttered under his breath, "Here comes more trouble."

Chapter Two

I frowned as I recognized the new arrival.

Sure, there had been a bit of buzz over the opening of another upscale deli slash diner a few months ago. It went by the folksy name of *Foodstock*, and its well-preserved raven-haired owner now made a beeline for Pierre.

I gave her full marks for energy and sass, and also for her pantsuit. Where Olivia Goodge fell flat, was on an ability to read the room. Although *Foodstock* had been unable to make a real dent in Pierre's business, Olivia had tried her best.

Rumor had it that she, together with her sidekick Katie, had copied Pierre's menu as best she could, and undercut his prices.

Since their arrival had coincided with my and Adriana's Italian vacation, I'd missed the opening battle, but according to my great-great-aunt's four-legged sources, the local animals steered clear of Olivia's bins.

Like most of the locals, the four-legged inhabitants also preferred Pierre's food.

But why did he seem so gloomy at seeing her in his place? He should be shrugging her competition off.

Olivia waved a glossy magazine at him. "Did you see that?"

"You too? My answer won't change. I'm not interested."

"It's a great opportunity for us together."

My shameless eavesdropping was cut short by a gaggle of women from the bridge club. These ladies, all in their fifties and sixties, were among Pierre's stalwarts. Thanks to Adriana's contributions to my gelato-making, they also formed a substantial part of my clientele.

"What's the flavor of the day?" their leader asked.

"Cherry and almond." I offered three regular flavors - vanilla with a twist, double chocolate with a hint of spice, and mint choc chip, together with two seasonal fruit-based ice creams, and one daily changing flavor.

So far, even at the end of September, I'd never had to return home with unsold gelato. Most of it tended to be gone when I left shortly after the high school kids came by. If some was by then left over, Pierre's wait staff took over my stall.

I was still busy with scooping gelato for the bridge ladies and for Neely Potts, a relative newcomer and one half of a vegetarian café, when Pierre was replaced by Fred Ward, one of my oldest friends in town.

Olivia dashed off, leaving the magazine behind.

Fred gave me a cheerful wave as he got ready to prepare the standing orders. He must have been the busiest retiree I'd ever met. Fred volunteered at the local library. He sat on the town council. He organized ball games for the children, and he also acted as a tour guide for the Cobblewood Cove museum, which held in its walls several mementos from the Darling family.

My ancestors had arrived here shortly after the Revolutionary War. Although we'd never been among the richest inhabitants, our name meant something on these shores.

My full name is Geneviève Darling Hepner, Genie for short. In my business dealings, I'd dropped my paternal name. Darling Designs sounded better. My first name came courtesy of my Francophile mother who'd shed her christened name of Amy for the much more sophisticated Aimée as soon as she and my dad had been sent by his bosses to Europe after their wedding.

They'd been happy moving from country to country and place to place for his career, and I'd been convinced I'd spent my life as a rolling stone too. But then, after ten years of widowhood, Aimée had not only married Tony Novak (with my full blessing!), she'd also rediscovered the delights of Cobblewood Cove.

So had I. What had started as a short visit, to sort out the ancestral home in a non-too-important small town at an equal distance from New York and Boston, had become my home for better or worse. There was something to be said for a place where everybody knew your name, if not your business.

Some of my family had achieved a certain amount of local fame. Among them was the "Dueling Darling", who was celebrated for successfully defending a lady's honor with his blade. That happened back in the days when sabers at noon were all the fashion.

Adriana's mother Rosalind had been nicknamed the "Daredevil Darling". She'd flown as a passenger in a flimsy aeroplane made of nothing but wood and canvas, ridden a Harley Davidson during the Great War until her worried husband had begged her not to make their children orphans, and she'd tirelessly marched and protested and lobbied for the women's vote.

I'd come close to following in their footsteps as the "Deranged Darling", until Adriana and I had worked out a way of interacting that didn't include me having a public discussion with what to everyone else appeared to be thin air.

Even now I sometimes forgot that she wasn't made of flesh and blood.

"Hey, girlfriend." Jolene, local girl Friday and the best handywoman on the whole East Coast, popped up in front of me. She practically ran the *Nuts and Bolts*, her family's hardware store, when she wasn't busy fixing electricity, plumbing, or other important jobs around town. Her connections reached to all layers of society.

If anything happened in Cobblewood Cove without her knowing, it would be a first. Adriana was the one thing Jolene was clueless about.

"Your usual?" Instead of waiting for an answer, I grabbed one of Jilly's gelato bowls and filled it with a scoop each of chocolate and the cherry and almond. Jolene had been my guinea pig for our creations and as such earned free gelato for life.

The same went for Jilly's pottery. The hardware store had been the first to promote her, and Jolene had introduced my friend to Kenji too.

She dipped in a spoon and swooned. "Every time I think I've hit my favorite combo, you strike again." She pointed at a shelf high above the food counter. On it sat more trophies than I'd ever seen outside the local sports club. "You should enter the competition at the fair. If this doesn't win, there is no justice in the world." She took another spoonful.

"Thanks, but I leave that to people who love public attention." There was no way on earth I'd do one of these events where you have to whip up your signature whatever in front of judges or any other audience. Having a ghost as your near-constant companion and business partner has its drawbacks, especially when she's the mastermind behind your success.

As much as Adriana deserved her creations to shine, I didn't trust myself to work together with her with too much attention on my every move. I made a mental note to make my great-great-aunt stay out of this particular loop. The road to trouble was paved with too much information.

Jolene handed me her empty bowl. "I've actually dropped by to ask if you need a cat sitter for tonight. Or is Aimée back in town?"

"You're a star but I think Cleo can handle a night on her own if I leave her enough food." I didn't mention that Cleo already had a sitter and that I was pretty sure cat and ghost had a ball whenever I was gone for a few hours.

"My offer stands," Jolene said. "I'll swing by before you leave, anyway. Your new lampshade should come this afternoon." With that, she headed for the door, and our rush hour began.

I'd expected Pierre to help Fred once he'd finished turning good honest food into something that changed your tastebuds forever. Instead, I saw him head towards the fire door that led to the staircase up to his private apartment. That was another break with routine.

"Is everything okay with Pierre?" I asked Fred as I stacked the dishwasher with my dirty bowls and cutlery. The six gloriously empty gelato containers would go home with me.

Drat. I'd forgotten that Jilly had given me a lift. Under normal circumstances, the Darling Villa was only a leisurely stroll away, past brownstone mansions and clapboard homes in white or shades of pastel. Carrying a tower of containers each capable of holding two gallons of ice cream would turn the distance of one mile into a challenge. I tried stacking the tubs this and that way, but they remained awkward.

Fred gave me a hand but didn't fare better. "Pierre's feeling a bit rough, that's all," he answered my question after a longish pause.

"Surely this isn't about the business with the flyers?"

For the last week, every single business in town that sold animal products had found posters taped to their doors, accusing them of murder. Neely Potts and her daughter Sallie, who owned the *Carrot Cove*, a vegetarian café at the end of Main Street, had been everyone's favorite suspects until a disgruntled ex-employee of the local butcher's had confessed to the prank.

Fred's mouth tightened. "This is strictly between you and me and the lamppost, but somebody has broken into the spare cash drawer in his office."

No wonder Pierre was down in the dumps. "Did they steal much?"

"At the most, fifty bucks. It's not the money he cares about. It's tough on him not having a clue who the burglar is."

"Did he call the police?" I already knew the answer. Pierre wouldn't dream of neglecting what he saw as his civic duty.

Fred confirmed that. "Not much they can do, they told him. You'll keep your eyes and ears open, won't you Genie? It's been a bit of a shock for him. Us old folks aren't as elastic as you anymore, but don't tell him I said that."

"Your secret's safe with me," I promised. While I wrestled some more with my containers, I wondered if I should check in on Pierre, but maybe he needed to be alone for a while. In the end, I settled on leaving the gelato containers behind, in Pierre's giant dishwasher. I had more at home.

The sun peeked through clouds as I left through the back door, catching a partial glimpse of Steve.

Most of him was hidden behind the potted trees Pierre had planted to cover the dumpsters. Steve's chef's jacket gave him away. A tendril of smoke curled up in the air. No, not smoke. I took a sniff. He was vaping, a habit I thought he'd quit.

Or maybe his companion was, for now, I also spotted a sneaker sticking out at an angle. The foot couldn't belong to Steve unless he was a secret contortionist, and his fiancée stuck to high heels.

I shrugged it off and went my merry way, for once alone and unencumbered.

The walk should have been bliss. Honeysuckle scented the warm air, bees darted in and out of the flowers, and a gentle breeze caressed my face. The shop windows shone, and behind the plate glass lay craft and art supplies, candles, and antiques. The cliffs and the cove were a little over a mile away, but if I turned my nose in the wind, I caught a whiff of salty sea air that added a certain sharpness to the mix.

Only two things prevented me from enjoying myself.

The first one was the break-in at Pierre's. Ten years ago, I'd have put my money on a couple of cash-strapped teenagers who'd had a few beers too many. Nowadays, they all paid electronically. I could count the occasions on one hand when someone younger than 30 had paid me in cash. So, who would commit a crime for a handful of dollars?

The other fly in the ointment was my missing companion. My path took me along the homes of some of Adriana's most fervent four-legged admirers, and they all made it clear they missed her.

The barking was bad enough, but worse was the sad, unblinking eyes that could have broken a heart of stone.

"I'll bring her soon," I promised every single dog. "I won't forget."

CHAPTER THREE

"So, what are you going to do?" Adriana asked before I so much as had hung up my jacket.

"Good afternoon to you, too." I stroked Cleo's head.

My great-great-aunt pushed out her bottom lip, in her sternest manner.

I glanced at the TV. On the screen, Adriana's perennial crush, Cary Grant, flirted with Constance Bennett. One of my roommate's most useful and also frustrating abilities included interrupting electricity, so she could start and pause DVDs and audiobooks generously supplied by me.

"Looks like you had a great day," I said.

She kept silent.

"You and Cleo can do whatever you want while I'm gone. I'm sure you'll love it," I said.

"That's not the point."

My heart sank. She was right. I was about to admit it when my phone pinged.

Adriana craned her neck to see who had sent me a message. "It's your beau."

I turned away. Matt Blake, art and museum security expert and my boyfriend of four months, had the distinction of feeling a pleasant, warm, and fuzzy sensation in Adriana's company.

He had no idea why, just like he had no idea that he came second on her list of heartthrobs, topped only by Cary Grant.

He also had no clue that he was the cause of the current strain on the Darling household. We'd dealt with privacy issues soon enough, so Adriana knew when entering my bedroom was okay and when I expected her to stay out of my room.

What she struggled with was the fact that I kept mum about her. That also meant that I preferred to leave town to spend some quality time with my boyfriend, leaving her behind.

Technically we'd found a way for her to roam, as long as she drew strength from various objects connected to her life, and from my presence. Staying home without me didn't hurt her either, because she was deeply connected to the building. It only hurt her feelings to be unacknowledged.

I read Matt's message. "Called away on business. Back Monday. Sorry xx"

Relief fought with disappointment. I'd looked forward to seeing him. But it also meant I didn't have to decide what or what not to say. If I told Matt I shared my life with my newly returned, corporeally challenged great-great-aunt, he might run for the hills. It would be a logical reaction.

On the other hand, Adriana was right that a real relationship demanded coming clean. If he declined to accept the fact that I had a ghost, we weren't meant to be.

We'd been discussing the issue for weeks now. I'd come close to talking to Matt a dozen times, only to chicken out.

Adriana tried to sneak up behind me.

I closed the message.

"How long will you be gone?" She put up her best attempt of putting on a brave face. The world had lost a great actor when she died, or maybe it was the steady diet of classic 1930s movies I fed her that inspired her acting skills.

"Well . . ." I paused. If I told her Matt had canceled, she'd think she'd have to entertain me all weekend to make up for it, which could be exhausting.

The doorbell chimed while I still debated with myself.

With a whoop of delight, Adriana slid down the railing.

"Wait till I open the door," I said to no one in particular. I had no means of comparison because my great-great-aunt was the only ghost I'd met, and I hoped with all my heart it would stay that way. What I knew from experience was that her energy and her powers were connected both to this house and to my person.

When I first met her on a fateful night in spring, she'd worn a silver evening frock that clung to her in all the right places - the same dress she had on when she met with an accident that ultimately led to her death. Un-wrinkled and flattering in a way sadly out of my league, that dress was what she wore day in, day out.

I suspected she'd been murdered, but without real proof we considered the case closed.

At least, she did. I had a hunch that her death and her reappearance after close to a century of nothingness might be connected to a missing necklace. If we found that, I assumed that we'd get our answers.

I also suspected she'd then be able to cross over what-ever threshold lay between my sphere and hers. Until that day, we were on a mission to recover as many of her former possessions as possible. She owned anoth-er evening gown, a little black dress designed by none other than Coco Chanel herself.

The Chanel frock now hung wrapped in a protective cover in an old wardrobe that had once belonged to Adriana, in a room as closely restored to its appearance in the Roaring Twenties as possible. She only put the little black dress on for special occasions, like a night at the theater or when we had a cocktail evening.

Technically the dress, which her adored older sister Belle had brought home for her from Chanel's shop in Paris, never left the wardrobe, but whatever she did, she could also wear it and gain strength and vitality.

For her, swishing through closed doors came easy when she felt full of juice and excitement, like now. For me, it never failed to give me a jolt.

I raced after her before I found out if she possessed enough energy to unlock the front door.

"Easy, sister," she admonished me as I came to a full stop. "You don't want to scare away folks because you've gone all tomatoey in your face."

As tempting as it was, I resisted the urge to come back with a snappy retort to her unflattering description of my appearance, and not only because I couldn't think of one.

Adriana predated me by generations, but in reality, I was a good ten years older, and even in my best days, I hadn't come close to matching her radiant beauty.

"Aren't you going to open?" she asked. "Or do you want me to have a gander who it is?"

"No." I shooed her away from the door before I let our visitor in.

"Tadah!" Jolene held a sturdy box. "It's a beauty. I wish I had the place to go with it."

I ushered her inside, and upstairs. Jolene had done most of the renovation work on the rooms.

The longtime inhabitant preceding me had been a great-aunt obsessed with quilting, tapestry, and other handicrafts, and her creations took over pretty much every nook and cranny. When she went to her heavenly reward, the Darling villa had required serious updating.

My mother, imaginative as always, had been able to come up with a mix of Japanese zen and Parisian flair for her apartment.

My own rooms paid full homage to Art Deco, for Adriana's sake.

Neither Aimée nor Jolene had batted an eyelid. They'd chalked my choice of interior design up as part of my fascination with that period, which was reflected in my jewelry designs. The glass lampshade in green, gold, and blue, which Jolene had sourced from wherever she found everything a customer asked for, would go on my landing. It echoed the dominant colors of my living room, where a peacock motif oozed period elegance.

"I'll hang it up for you," she offered. "You'll probably want to get ready for your date night."

Adriana gave me a brave little smile.

Cleo slunk around her ankles and gave me the cold shoulder, or whatever the cat equivalent was.

I kept my cool. "There's no need to hurry," I said. "There's been a change of plans."

Jolene whistled through her teeth. "That cousin of mine better behave himself."

"Matt is fine," I told her before her imagination could run wild. Or Adriana's. "He's been called away on a job."

"That means you're free tonight?"

"We certainly are," my great-great-aunt said and nodded enthusiastically. Her perfectly waved blonde hair gently moved and her blue eyes sparkled. Of the two of us, Adriana was the social butterfly. She had a lot of catching up to do, after all.

"What do you have in mind?" I asked Jolene. Experience had taught me not to blindly say yes any longer. Before I hardened my heart, I'd been dragged to a rave we both hated (Jilly) and a wild swim that ended with me being bitten by all the insects that lived in the river (again, Jilly).

Jolene was no better. Last month she'd taken me to a bar twenty miles away, where the band was so loud, we both fled before our ear drums burst. It turned out, Jolene had been asked to overhaul the bar's complete wiring, including the sound system, and had wanted to check it out for herself.

She probably remembered my graphic reaction to that night, because she said, "I thought, pizza and music? It's going to be fine, I promise."

Adriana clapped her hands. "Swell. Just us girls, cutting a rug in a classy joint." She did a few dance steps.

I gave in. "I'll pick you up after I've dropped off tomorrow's gelato at Pierre's." That agreed, I left Jolene to install the lamp shade and a buzzer system, while Adriana and I took care of our business.

Gem and Gelato was too young to risk losing customers, so they could purchase the ice cream at Pierre's Mondays to Sundays, although I took the weekends off. Thanks to a huge freezer in the revamped garage I only had the flavor of the day to finish, before the gelato was churned for the last time.

Adriana swung her arms, windmill-fashion, beside me. "What do you think where she's taking us? I wish they'd kept the speakeasies open. I miss the old joints. You never knew what was going to happen." She mimed rat-a-tat-tatting a machine gun. "Chicago overcoat, anyone?"

I chuckled. It was a safe bet Adriana had never had a close encounter with the mob, no matter what she said.

Sure, Cobblewood Cove had had its bootleggers and rum runners, and its own speakeasy right here in town which until recently had housed a bar. One ramshackle house on the cliffs was supposed to have housed a gambling den, among other illegal entertainment. In comparison to the colorful past of places like Chicago though, Cobblewood Cove's own history could at the most be called sepia-tinted.

Adriana herself also exuded a certain flair of innocence, despite her penchant for hard-boiled slang, taken directly from her beloved old pulp fiction magazines. Since she'd also adopted a few more modern expressions, she only peppered her speech with period expressions when something excited her - like a night out.

With half an hour to spare, I set off for Pierre's, the gelato containers in the boot of my old Toyota and my great-great-aunt with her feet propped up on the dashboard. "Take them down," I ordered. "Otherwise I'll drop you straight back home before Jolene and I go out. Including your brick."

The chunk of masonry from the villa's basement allowed her to venture out with me to our heart's content. I'd put it in a cardboard box in my purse, to prevent questions about why I carried it around.

Adriana pouted. "You wouldn't be so mean." Still, she obeyed.

I allowed myself a smug little grin. When it came to dealing with my great-great-aunt, every little victory counted.

I left her standing outside *Butler's Pantry*, chatting away to one of the dogs who'd earlier given me the sad-eye treatment. That should keep her happy and out of trouble.

I let myself in through the service entrance at the back. It should all have been silent, apart from the muted music that was part and parcel of Pierre's evenings.

Not tonight though. Instead of Dolly Parton and the Beach Boys, a man's voice cut through the silence. "You'll never receive another offer like this."

Pierre answered in a cold tone. "I'm not selling, and that's final."

"You're throwing away a small fortune, and for what? You have no kids, nobody's here to take over apart from me, which is not going to happen, and you're not getting any younger. Whereas if you agree to my plan, we'll both be happy."

"I wouldn't worry about *Butler's Pantry*. Everything is sorted and fixed, black on white. Now if you'll excuse me --" Pierre's apartment door slammed.

I fled through to the shop room. I didn't want him to think I'd spied on him. I counted to one minute under my breath until I thought it safe to go back and fetch the rest of the containers I'd stacked up outside.

"Genie?" His voice startled me. I hadn't heard his steps.

"Oh, hi, Pierre." I rearranged my countenance into an innocent grin. It was meant to show him that I had not listened to anything at all. Then I got a closer look at him. His hands were shaking slightly, and his bushy brows knitted furiously together. "Are you okay?" What a stupid question, I told myself, and yet I had no idea what else to say.

"People are vultures," he said. "Always wanting something else from you, until they've picked your bones clean and they can throw you out with the trash."

That sounded worse than I'd expected. I only hoped people did not include me.

He gave me a brief pat on the back. "Ignore an old man. Now you go and have fun. I'll be fine in the morning." He fluttered his hands at me and I had no choice but to leave.

Adriana peeled away from her canine buddy as soon as I came out and joined her. "What took you so long?"

I rarely lied to her, but Pierre deserved his privacy. So, I said, "Nothing."

Chapter Four

Jolene insisted on leaving my car at her house and riding in hers. She'd gone all out on this outing, with a sequinned top, a skirt that showed off her waist, and her long hair in a loose updo. Her plateau wedges combined chic and comfort. At least that had been the claim at the shoe store, she told me.

Adriana gave her an approving smile.

I didn't fare as well in her opinion, despite my smart blazer over black pants and white shirt.

"Just because you've snagged Matt you don't have to give up on getting all dolled up once in a blue moon," she admonished me.

"I haven't," I protested.

"You haven't what?" Jolene, blissfully unaware of our fashion critic's presence, asked.

"I haven't figured out where we're going. Looking at you, I feel underdressed."

She giggled. "No need. I just needed a change from coveralls and work boots."

I heard the soft music before I saw our destination. *Vine and Vinyl* was the town's latest addition to boutique shops using alliterations. Jolene nodded left and right to people as she led us inside.

The store belonged to the same building that housed *Foodstock*, and the two businesses could be turned into one giant room via a large sliding door.

A small stage at the back held a baby grand. Playing a Gershwin medley was a man about my age, with a shock full of dark hair and a rapt expression.

Jolene planted herself at our table without taking her gaze off the stage.

"He's swell," Adriana marveled. "Why didn't we come here sooner?" I

had the same question unless Jolene'd feared it would be disloyal to Pierre, since *Vine and Vinyl* only offered a bar and a few tables. More seating and food, including the promised pizza, came courtesy of *Foodstock*. The connecting folding doors had been fully opened for tonight.

Jolene grinned. "Not too bad, is it?"

The pianist looked up and spotted her. He missed a note.

I opened the drinks menu. "What would you like? Wine, or a wine cocktail? They also have tap beer."

Adriana shuddered. It only took a few deep breaths for her to become tipsy on alcohol fumes, but she drew a line at lager and ale. "Giggle-water for me, please."

I raised an eyebrow at her. Champagne and prosecco were a surefire way for her to lose control in a twinkle.

She glanced around, honing in on the other customers. "Hotsy-totsy, the gang's all here," she declared and sashayed over to the *Foodstock* side where our old friends, the Schuyler sisters, and our girlfriend and town librarian, Daphne Mills, applauded the pianist. Daphne was around my age, with snazzy spectacles and wild hair.

"I'd like something classy, that sets the right tone," Jolene said to me. "You choose."

I headed for the bar. "A spritzer and a frosé please," I said to the bartender.

Someone jostled me, and I moved out of the way, making a half-turn as I did so.

Snippets of conversations drifted past. I barely listened, distracted by a woman I'd seen making her way through the swing doors that led to *Foodstock*'s kitchen. Katie again, only with hunched shoulders and no raised fist.

"I'm sure you'll win the competition," a shrill voice said in one corner. "Forget that old fraud Pierre, you don't need him. Talk about a rotten apple not falling far from the tree."

Before I could see who did the talking, or who their words were aimed at, the bartender put down my drinks.

I picked up the glasses and carefully balanced them as I weaved my way through the increasingly crowded room.

Primrose Schuyler beckoned me over. "Genie, sweetheart." I

inched towards her and her companions. Jolene had already joined them, but Adriana was nowhere to be seen.

Not good. The last thing I needed was an unsupervised ghost cutting loose in a bar.

Daphne pulled up a chair for me. In the background, the music started again.

Both Primrose and Dahlia beamed at me and raised their white wine glasses in a silent toast. Today, they'd decided on matching blue dresses. Since they'd also both decided to go all natural with their matching silver hairdos, it needed experience to tell them apart. They might be in their late seventies, but in Cobblewood Cove's hierarchy, they were the first ladies. The influx of new families lured by the wholesome atmosphere of a coastal town, which still was within easy reach of the big cities, hadn't changed that.

"We've told Daphne how you saved our little Petey," Dahlia said.

"And how your ice cream has become our favorite dessert." Primrose twinkled at me.

"Even our nephew can't get enough," Dahlia said. "He doesn't usually have a sweet tooth, but there's something irresistible about those flavors." She lowered her voice. "We'd never ask you to share your secrets, of course, but we wondered if you'd be kind enough to create a signature ice cream for our parties, something with edible flowers if they're suitable?"

"I'll see what I can do. Both primroses and dahlias are safe to eat, I believe." Part of me wondered if they tried to throw more business my way, without being too obvious.

They didn't have to. They didn't know, but I'd forever be in their debt. Without the sisters, I might never have met Matt, or been able to reclaim those precious items that my great-great-aunt relied on. Like the Chanel dress she'd chosen for tonight. Also, even without owing the Schuylers a debt of gratitude, I'd have been inclined to fulfill their wish, because both sisters were as kind as they came. Daphne cocked her head as I scanned the room for my elusive relative. For an instant, I thought I spotted her, next to the baby grand. .

"Listen," Daphne said. "Who is that singer?"

I closed my eyes. A full-throated soprano made itself heard despite the chatter of the few who'd come in the first place to dine.

"It's probably a record," Daphne declared. "Bessie Smith maybe?"

That was correct, as the pianist confirmed at this very moment.

But I heard another voice, too, a softer, sweeter one, and one I knew only too well.

Adriana Darling had decided to become the belle of the ball and draped herself across the baby grand.

The pianist wiped his brow. It could have been just the heat from the crowd and his exertion. Or he could have fallen under Adriana's spell.

I excused myself and moved closer to my great-great-aunt. It was great to see her having a good time. It would be less great if she enjoyed herself too much. On those occasions, she tended to make light-bulbs shatter and fuses blow. Given the amount of sconces and chandeliers, I shuddered to think about the dangers involved.

Adriana leaned back on one elbow and gazed soulfully at the pianist. "Play me another tune," she crooned.

I glared at her.

She fluffed her hair and flattered her lashes at the musician, who broke into an old Cole Porter song I knew Adriana adored. We'd been dancing to it until my feet hurt.

Judging by the surprised looks from the bar, it wasn't something he often played. I shrugged it off. If I had to contemplate the idea that in addition to all her other talents my great-great-aunt also could bend minds to her will, the thought would drive me to the nearest shrink. As it was, I counted myself lucky that so far I'd been spared the straitjacket and padded walls.

Daphne waved at a newcomer. "Here we are." She signaled to the waitress who carried platters of cheese, cold cuts, and assorted nibbles past us. "Could we get one of those platters, the cheesy fries, and two quattro stagione pizzas?"

Jolene kept watching the pianist who in return kept glancing in our direction when he wasn't too busy with his sheet music.

Did I detect a budding romance? That would explain why she'd dressed up to come here.

Fred Ward squeezed himself in with us.

Adriana hopped off the piano and joined us for an enthusiastic sniff of my spritzer. "This joint is hopping," she said. "And that ivory tinkler is hot stuff. Pity there is no space here to really cut a rug." She gave Jolene a knowing grin.

So I had been right. My great-great-aunt had also picked up on the tension between those two.

Jolene studied the ceiling with a critical eye.

"Your work?" I asked.

She snorted. "They brought in some fancy big city contractor, courtesy of the partner." She gave the molding and the ceiling rosette a crushing stare.

Adriana lost interest. She'd spotted a table at the far end, with crates of vinyl records and CDs stored underneath. An old gramophone sat on top, with just enough space next to it for a very agile, fleet-footed dancer - or a Charleston-loving ghost.

I paid little attention to the conversation going on around me until Fred said something and Daphne gave me a gentle poke with her elbow. "Sorry," I said. "What did you say?"

"It's too loud here for a proper conversation," Fred agreed. "I was only saying that I wouldn't mention this little outing to Pierre."

Jolene coughed as her drink went down the wrong pipe.

"Why not?" Daphne asked. She paused until the waitress had dropped off our oder and left, before she continued. "Don't say this place is hurting his profits." She helped herself to cheesy fries, something that Pierre didn't offer.

Jolene crammed a stuffed mushroom into her mouth and chewed it deliberately. "Nice, but not even close to Pierre's," she declared.

I found myself the center of their attention. "Whenever I'm there, Pierre's place is buzzing," I said.

"It's not the bottom line that's bugging him," Fred said. "It's folks." He mimed zipping his lips as Olivia and Katie came in sight.

Before I'd the chance to mull this over, I heard a triumphant yell and saw my great-great-aunt, literally swinging from the chandelier. I prayed that nobody else noticed the gentle movement above our heads, and that, as a specter, Adriana was not able to rip the light fixture right off.

The pianist took a break, and Jolene strolled over to chat with him.

Adriana still dangled from the chandelier.

Daphne held her glass up and signaled that she wanted a top-up. "Make this so dirty you'll need a clean-up crew," she said to the waitress.

Adriana somersaulted to the ground, narrowly missing the Schuyler sisters who'd decided to call it a night. She made a bee-line for Daphne's drink.

I glowered at her. No wonder she was in a high old mood. Where I'd prudently kept the alcohol in my spritzer to a mere splash, Adriana had been fueling up on our librarian's booze. Wine might have been the base, but vodka and a dash of absinthe made for a potent combination.

Daphne caught my expression and misinterpreted it. "Have I done something wrong?"

I gave her a reassuring head shake.

Adriana wiggled her hips. "Don't be such a stick in the mud. This town needs a bit of shaking up."

I massaged my temple. I could feel a ghost-induced headache coming on.

Fred peered at me. "Is everything alright?"

"Oh, yes." His concern touched me.

Adriana flung herself theatrically on a chair - one at a table occupied by Steve. I hadn't noticed him or his fiancée, a dainty brunette called Tammy Lee, before. She had a firm grasp on Steve and a fondness for luxury at odds with his chef's income, which she demonstrated nicely with the bottle of Dom Perignon in a cooler.

Katie gave her a small wave and a thumbs-up.

Tammy waved back, with a hint of a smile before a tiny frown again marred her skilfully made-up features.

A chuckle escaped me because Adriana leaned over to tickle the fiancée's chin.

Tammy scratched the spot.

Adriana winked at me. I let my face go blank. The last thing my incorrigible relative needed was encouragement. Still, since to the best of my knowledge I had never seen the fiancée other than in a pouty mode, I didn't begrudge Adriana her fun.

Tammy tapped her red talons on a glossy magazine. With every inaudible word she spoke, Steve shrunk deeper into his seat.

The pianist, on the other hand, grinned so hard it was infectious as Jolene led him over to us. "Everyone, this is Felix, owner, and mastermind behind this venue," she said.

"You're flattering me." He introduced himself to each of us separately. His handshake lasted just long enough to be personal without being overpowering. Up close, he had a few more crinkles around the eyes than I'd expected.

I adjusted my impression from early to late thirties.

He included us all in a warm smile. "I hope you enjoy yourself. My sister Olivia and I have been overwhelmed with the friendliness of our new neighbors."

Olivia Goodge was his sister?

Jolene gave me a little shrug and a sign to maybe not mention her criticism of the workmanship involved with the venue.

Daphne studied Felix, from his tousled locks to the well-cut suit and white shirt.

I could almost read her mind, classy, but not overdone. I agreed. Felix seemed nice enough, and considering that the dating pool in Cobblewood Cove for people our age could only be called a trickle, I was thrilled for Jolene.

Adriana had tired of Steve and his Tammy. She floated back to us in a zigzag. Her shoes didn't touch the ground, a sure sign that she had crossed the line from tipsy and fully entered sloshed territory. She collided with Felix's sister, who sat down with Steve and Tammy. The poor guy turned pink in the face as both women moved in on him.

I had to get my great-great-aunt under control.

"You're leaving already?" Daphne asked. She swigged her cocktail with all signs of enjoyment. "Come on, stay, it's the only show in town."

Sad, but true. One of Cobblewood Cove's charms lay in the lack of rowdy establishments. On the flip side, there weren't too many sophisticated places open after ten pm.

The one bar in town had closed a few months back after the owner decided he preferred the Californian sun. Both *Foodstock* and *Vine and Vinyl* were part of a new rejuvenation wave in town, sparked by a new building estate as well as a week-long food and craft fair that would bring in visitors from all over the state in a week's time.

"I'll come with you," Jolene said. She gave Felix a last, lingering glance as he returned to his baby grand.

"What do you think?" she asked on our way to her place.

"Think of what?" I tried to grab hold of Adriana's shawl or at least its spiritual copy, but I might as well have attempted to catch fog.Thn I caught on to Jolene. "Oh, Felix. I liked him. The place has a lot of potential, too."

"I thought, if their business picks up, he'll need a bigger space. Remember that empty bar where the old speakeasy was?"

Adriana's peepers grew saucer-wide. "That'd be swell," she said. "He could have hooch and hoofers, and I'd teach you how to paint the town red." She twirled around, setting all the neighborhood dogs off for a round of questioning woofs and yips.

"It wouldn't take much to spruce it up. The bones are still good, and we could have themed nights for dances." Jolene linked arms with me.

"You've given it a lot of thought," I said. "How long have you known Felix?"

She hesitated. "You won't tell anyone?"

"Just spill the beans," Adriana demanded.

I crossed my heart.

"I met him online, last year. Friend of a friend thing. He asked me about Cobblewood Cove because they were searching for a small town to set up shop."

"But then why didn't Olivia hire you to do the renovation?" I wondered.

"She or rather her business partner already had a guy lined up, like I said. But this has to stay between us, okay? I don't want Pierre to be mad at me for bringing them here."

She needn't have worried. When I next saw Pierre, he would never be upset with anyone, ever again.

Chapter Five

I arrived early that Monday morning.

Adriana had been on her most thoughtful behavior for the rest of the weekend. She and Cleo had let me sleep in on Sunday, and we'd spent a few peaceful hours trying out new gelato recipes. I was no Pierre, so I kept notes on every single batch we cooked up and rated them separately.

We'd just finished when my phone rang and my mother announced her imminent arrival. Although she owned the house, I acted as caretaker. The rent money she wouldn't dream of accepting, I put into improvements, like the new lampshade.

Because Aimée and her husband had originally planned to stay away for another week, I spent the rest of the Sunday evening dusting, plumping pillows, and arranging flowers in vases.

Outside, rain poured down and strong winds rattled our shutters so badly, that Cleo hid under the bed.

I woke to a serene day, with azure skies, cotton candy clouds, and the noises of my mother and her husband unpacking.

I was scheduled to man *Gem and Gelato* until the late afternoon on Mondays, but I hoped Pierre would agree to have his help cover for me if I assisted with the food prep in his kitchen.

The back door to *Butler's Pantry* was open, which saved me fishing for my keys. They tended to get lost in the depths of my purse, which I hoped to organize one day. Inside, everything was silent.

I stored my containers in the freezer and took out the smaller tubs I used at my ice cream station. The empty tubs I'd left over the weekend stood on a trolley, ready to be wheeled to my car.

When I returned, there still was no sign of Pierre and not a peep from his apartment upstairs.

Maybe he'd been taken ill, or he'd had a fall, I thought with a growing sense of unease. Spry as he was, at his age he was physically vulnerable. I rummaged in my purse for the key to unlock the connecting door to the staircase.

Upstairs, everything was quiet as I knocked on Pierre's door. He'd given me a spare key for emergencies, so I let myself in.

At first glance, the living room looked as it should, clean and cozy. Only the mat by the balcony showed parts of a sole profile.

Then my breath caught in my chest so hard it hurt.

The wall safe gaped open, and behind the sofa, a socked foot poked out, horribly still. My stomach lurched as I forced myself to move closer.

Pierre was lying face-down on the rug.

I didn't need to see the blood stains to be sure he was dead.

Icy fingers crept over my spine. This couldn't be true.

Any moment now he'd push himself off the ground. He'd shake his head at the stains on his carpet by the balcony door and brainstorm with me what dishes in this week's menu would compliment my flavors of the day.

Any moment now.

That moment didn't come.

The next thing I registered after I'd dialed 911, was a blanket being wrapped around my shoulders and the concerned voice of a paramedic talking to two other people.

I blinked. The blur cleared and my eyes could focus again. I looked anywhere but towards the rug. My gaze fastened on two police officers, one short and one tall.

"Ms Darling," the taller one said, as if Officer Hank Newby and his partner, Officer Tilda Ramos, hadn't long since stopped the formalities. Hank was Jolene's cousin, and this was a small town.

Officer Ramos touched my shoulder. "Are you up for a few questions, Ms Darling?" She handed me a tissue to wipe away tears I hadn't noticed before.

I dried my face. "Of course, only there's not much to tell you."

Hank Newby took me to the police station, while my old friend Pierre officially became a part of the homicide statistic.

Tilda Ramos followed in my Toyota. They'd both decided I wasn't fit to drive, yet.

I barely was able to, an hour later, when I parked my car in our driveway. My teeth chattered and I fumbled on my way inside.

Aimée hugged me tight before I could do so much as close the door. "Oh, sweetheart."

I calmed down as I inhaled the smell of her perfume, mixed with freshly brewed coffee. Those were the familiar scents of my childhood when nothing bad could happen as long as I had my mother.

I'd dealt with murder before, but this one was personal, and it hurt.

Pierre had been my friend. He'd taken me in with my fledgling business and supported me.

I shivered. Hopefully, Officers Newby and Ramos had clapped the handcuffs on the culprit already. Anything else was unbearable to consider.

Cleo raced down the staircase and rubbed herself against my legs.

Aimée gave me a big squeeze and let me go so I could scoop the cat up and bury my face in her soft fur.

"I thought you'd locked your door so this one couldn't escape." My mother petted what little she could reach of Cleo who broke into a full-throated purr.

"Obviously you needed her," my great-great-aunt said.

I should have known that Adriana wouldn't stay away. Her features were filled with sadness and sympathy.

"I must have forgotten to close the door properly," I said. Claiming that Cleo had figured out how to work door handles might have satisfied Aimée's curiosity, but it would also give her new reasons to worry.

As for telling her that a dear, not quite departed relative could at a push muster enough strength to move objects might have pushed my mother over the edge.

She led me to the kitchen and poured me a coffee strong enough to compete in its own Olympics. She, and to my surprise Adriana as well, kept quiet long enough for me to drink in peace and compose myself.

"How did you know about Pierre?" I asked.

Aimée's hands were unsteady as she poured herself a cup. "Jolene called me."

Of course. Jolene's relationship with the local grapevine resembled an umbilical cord.

"She said you've been questioned by the police." Deep worry lines appeared on Aimée's normally youthful face, giving me a glimpse of how she'd look as an old woman. "I hope they won't suspect you."

"They wouldn't. Nobody could be that stupid." Adriana perched herself on top of the table.

My head whirled. "No, of course not. I mean, why should I want to hurt Pierre?"

"Why would anyone?" Aimée asked.

True. "I need a lie-down," I said.

"Do you want me to stay with you?" My mother stroked my cheek.

Adriana shook her head at me. I managed a wan smile. "I'll just cuddle up with Cleo and sleep for a bit."

"Call me if you need anything." Aimée clutched her throat. "This town used to be so peaceful, and now this, after that horrible murder in spring - I wonder if we should stay."

Now it was my turn to hug her for comfort. "Statistically speaking, Cobblewood Cove is still ranking at the bottom for violent crime. I'm sure this will all be solved in a day or two. If on the other hand, Miss Marple or Jessica Fletcher move to town, we'll run for the hills."

This made Aimée chuckle as planned.

Adriana gave me a non-comprehensive stare.

I'd forgotten that she'd not yet been acquainted with the famous lady detectives. I put them on my mental list for her entertainment but that would have to wait.

I curled up on my bed, with cat and ghost by my side, and my phone at my fingertips, willing it to ring and inform me that, indeed, an arrest had been made, and all residents of our beautiful town could be at ease.

I drifted off to sleep when Adriana whispered in my ear. "Do you think the police already know who killed our dearest Pierre? Or do we have to take over again?"

Chapter Six

A rough tongue flickered over my hand.

I pulled it away.

A growl pierced the silence.

I gave up and opened my eyes.

Adriana stood in front of me, hands on her hips and a stern frown on her features. "Enough with the moping," she said. "Isn't it time we do something?"

"Like what?"

She sighed. "What we always do. You and I, we're like private eyes, gumshoes, the best gosh-darn operators in the whole country, if you ask me. Unless the police have got our guy in behind bars, we're not going to let the thug who did away with a friend get away with it."

Cleo meowed her agreement.

I did nothing of the sort. "We'll need to give the police a day or two," I said. "I'm certain they'll solve this murder like that." I snapped my fingers for illustration.

"While we just stand by and twiddle our thumbs?" Adriana sounded disappointed.

"Yes." I hugged myself. "I wish I'd never gone up there." Try as I might, I couldn't unsee the body on the rug. "The police know all the players, and they'll be under a lot of pressure to find the murderer. Everybody loved Pierre."

Everybody, except for one person.

"You don't believe that yourself, do you?" Adriana asked.

I felt tears welling up.

She relented. "What you need is a hot meal and a snifter of brandy."

Cleo touched my leg with her paw.

"And something good for Cleo. Her tummy's as hollow as a drum," Adriana added.

A plaintive noise made it clear that action was indeed needed if the poor tabby was to be saved from starvation.

I rolled out of bed and headed for my small kitchen. Downstairs was a chef's paradise. Up here, I had enough space and equipment to rustle up decent meals. If I wanted to feed an army, I'd move to Aimée's kitchen.

Pierre had advised her on the design.

No, I told myself, I was not going to dwell on him.

Only a few sad morsels remained in Cleo's food bowls which I'd filled this very morning.

She must have wolfed her meal down too fast, which did not bode well. In the corner by the stove, where the mop had a hard time reaching, I spotted a telltale trail of gooey stuff.

"The news got to her," Adriana said. "You can't blame a cat for having a delicate system."

I stroked Cleo's head. The sun streamed through the window and made her orange fur glow like a sunset over the Tuscan hills.

Cleo's softness and warmth helped settle my own stomach too. Whatever happened, some things stayed the same, and some duties couldn't be neglected. Taking care of the cat was one of them.

Another thought hit me. What would happen to *Butler's Pantry* and with it, my business? I felt a pang of unease. It seemed indecent to think about my bottom line in this situation, but like everybody else, I needed my income. Deep in thought, I cleaned up Cleo's mess and refilled her bowls. "I need fresh air to clear my head," I told my companions.

Adriana's face lit up. "We're going to nose around?"

"No. I'll go for a walk, that's all." Cobblewood Cove was one of those small towns with wide sidewalks, where people who lived downtown could still move under their own steam without being considered eccentric.

Adriana whispered something in Cleo's ear.

The cat chirped in response.

"She says we should hurry, and she wants fresh chicken for dinner, after the shock," Adriana said.

They both gave me an identical look of trusting innocence that belonged on the cover of a magazine.

"It would be mean to say no," my resident pet-whisperer declared.

"What a lucky coincidence that the grocer's is next to *Butler's Pantry*."

"You're right. That is lucky." Adroana fluttered her lashes.

Aimée stopped me on the way out. "Do you want me to come along?"

"Thanks, but I'm fine."

"Are you sure?"

In the background, her husband called out. "If Genie needs you, she'll tell you."

"I will," I promised as I grabbed my coat from the rack in the hallway.

I forced my feet to move towards the square. On Pierre's shop door hung a closed sign, and parked outside was a police van. I walked straight past and headed for the bench on the green.

Small clusters of people huddled close by, but several hours after the discovery, most folks would either have been over the first shock or wait until the evening to meet and speculate.

Daphne came towards me. "Mind if I sit for a spell?"

I patted the seat beside me.

She gave me a concerned once-over. "How are you holding up? I've been told you were interviewed by the police. According to some, you narrowly avoided arrest."

"What utter baloney," Adriana exclaimed.

A grim chuckle escaped me. "I should have thought of that. Did they also tell you about how murderously I wield my gelato scoop?"

"Fred shut them up pretty quickly," Daphne said.

"He's a sweetheart," Adriana said. "I just want to know who's been bad-mouthing you."

I wondered the same.

"Nobody in their right mind would consider you as a suspect," Daphne said. "It's only people who have no clue, like Tammy."

"Steve's fiancée?" How charming, I thought.

"What do you reckon is going to happen to *Butler's Pantry*?" I asked Daphne. I remembered the argument I'd overheard, where Pierre had mentioned he'd made arrangements.

"No idea. There's his nephew, but Grayson's a veterinarian, not a chef. Steve might be keen to reopen the doors, if that's Grayson's wish."

My jaw dropped. "Reopen? Isn't everything locked up, as a crime scene?"

"Only until tomorrow or the day after, I've been told." She motioned towards the police van that just set off. "You'll have the biggest crowd on your hand you've ever dealt with, mark my words."

"Come for the gossip, stay for the gelato?" A sick taste crept into my mouth.

"Something like that. I only hope this'll be cleared up soon, before it spoils our festival week. Pierre has been one of the biggest supporters behind the scenes, and it's our chance to honor his memory." She squinted against the late afternoon sun. "I'd better run. Are we still on for tonight?"

I'd almost forgotten. Mondays had become girls' night, where Jolene, Daphne, and I took turns hosting each other. This week, I had hostess duties. I gave her a thumbs-up.

"Great. Don't let anybody get you down." With this, Daphne dashed back to her library, and Adriana reminded me of our urgent visit to the grocer's.

To spare me any more stress on this fateful day, my girlfriends came carrying food. The wine bottle in Jolene's bag had a sticker from *Vine and Vinyl*, but I refrained from mentioning it.

We'd all agreed that we needed to forget the sordid present and we'd talk about anything but Cobblewood Cove. As a result, we ran out of topics.

Even Adriana kept silent as she perched on the windowsill and gazed at the moon and the twinkling stars. Cleo lay next to her and snored gently.

"How about a game?" Jolene asked. Her gaze traveled to my entertainment area, which held all my old fashioned games. "We could do charades, or Monopoly, or Clue." She clapped a hand over her mouth. "Sorry."

"It's okay," I said. "We can pretend we don't want to talk about it, but actually, it's making it worse to have to watch our words among friends."

Daphne agreed. "It's unhealthy to bottle up trauma, especially for an eyewitness like you."

"My cousin Hank says they should soon be able to make an arrest," Jolene said.

"They do?" A huge weight plummeted off my shoulders. "I was afraid I might have destroyed clues although I didn't touch anything."

"Hank says it's pretty much an open and shut case, from what the detective in charge told him. They're only waiting for the autopsy report, I reckon. *Butler's Pantry* should be up and running again in no time at all."

Daphne raised her glass. "Here's to justice, and a return to normalcy in Cobblewood Cove."

"To justice." A huge sense of relief washed over me. I had my ghost, my friends, and no need to throw myself into yet another dangerous situation.

Maybe all would be well. I ignored the tiny voice in the back of my head that told me to have my noodle examined.

That voice sounded too much like a certain ghost.

CHAPTER SEVEN

An upset voice stopped me in my tracks.

Adriana used the opportunity to say hello to a puppy who sat unhappily strapped into a stroller.

"Three days, and what have the police done? We might all wake up in our beds, with our throats slit," one of the bridge club ladies complained to Officer Newby at the top of her lungs.

A pink tinge washed over his cheeks, making me pity him. "You have nothing to worry about, Ma'am."

"Says who? A good man, a valued pillar of the community, has been slain in his own home, and all you lot have done is sit on your backside and eat donuts."

Considering that Hank Newby and his partner had been doing their rounds on foot ever since I'd found Pierre's body, to make the townsfolk feel safe, these accusations were decidedly unjust.

They were also widely shared. People expected to see an arrest, and with every passing hour, the anxiety grew.

The loud lady pointed a ringed finger at me. At a glance, her jewels weighed in the region of four or five carats. For someone afraid of murder and mayhem, she flaunted a lot of wealth. She said, "Ask Genie Darling why she won't set foot in *Butler's Pantry* ever again. If a mere ice cream seller can't feel safe, how can we?"

Adriana hissed at her. "Mere ice cream seller? How dare you, you dumb Dora."

I decided to step in before my great-great-aunt decided to give the rude woman the icy treatment - literally. She could chill out people in a blink if she put her all into it. I said, "I only relocated to the *Cocoa Cabana* until Pierre's heirs have decided what they want to do. I'd love to be back where I started out."

What I said was true to a certain degree. The police had finished with Pierre's building, and officially everything was allowed to be open again, but the uncertainty remained. The heir apparent had already been seen out and about, but not by me.

I'd been too busy moving my cart and a few bar stools into my new location. The owner of Cobblewood Cove's premier café had invited me months ago, but Pierre had been my first choice.

Jolene had offered to help me with the final things needed for the relocation, under Officer Newby's watchful eye. That was the reason I stood here and why she appeared now.

My best guess was that Hank Newby intended to impress the big shots with his diligence since neither my cart nor I were under any kind of suspicion. At least that's what his partner had told me.

The bridge club lady grudgingly power-walked off in her pink velour tracksuit and purple sneakers.

Adriana stuck out her tongue at the woman.

I resisted the temptation to do the same.

Officer Newby mopped his brow with a handkerchief. "Folks are driving me crazy," he muttered. Then he realized that I'd heard him and colored again.

Jolene snickered at her cousin's discomfort and went to pick up the last box with my stuff.

"Don't think about it," I told him. "We're all a bit on edge."

"We'll catch our perp, you wait and see." The handkerchief came into play again. "I only hope it's fast enough before the chamber of commerce has a fit."

Officer Ramos held a paper bag with sandwiches as she joined us. "Hi, Genie. How are you holding up?" So, we were on a first-name basis again.

"I'd sleep better if all this was over," I said.

"Wouldn't we all?" She motioned her partner a few steps away from me.

I stayed where I was, making it unmissable that I had no intention to eavesdrop, on whatever Tilda Ramos had to say to her partner in private.

I didn't need to. I had my spy.

Adriana circled them, with a rapt expression. "Ooooh, that's a good one," she said. "Genie, brick me up."

With my foot, I shoved my purse with the masonry closer to her.

She touched it first and then she slid her hand into Tilda Ramos's uniform jacket. Adriana's cheeks bulged with the exertion, but she pushed on. When she finally exhaled, her hand held a folded piece of paper which she opened and dropped.

It fluttered onto the ground.

Adriana gave me a signal, and I called out, "You lost something, Officer Ramos."

Tilda picked up her note and peered at it with surprise. "I wonder how that could happen."

With Adriana in tow, I left her to puzzle.

"Not so fast," my great-great-aunt panted. Moving an object without proper preparation took its toll on her, no matter how light it was.

We legged it across the street.

The *Cocoa Cabana* ladies had kindly offered to take care of my gelato station, whenever I needed a break after my horrific experience. Today was my first day with them, and I hadn't intended to take them up on it, except that Adriana would probably spontaneously combust or disappear in a vapor if I let her stew on her discoveries.

Since she'd sworn on Cary Grant's soul that she'd keep her lips sealed when I had to interact in public, it would be cruel to deny her privacy.

To be honest, I was bursting to find out more. I quickly popped into the café to make arrangements.

The conversation stopped the instant I set foot inside. The last time I'd commanded this much undivided atten-tion, I'd drawn the winner of a weekend away with private catering for Pierre's first and last tombola in support of the animal rescue.

Adriana was still recovering when I returned to her. She basked in the sunshine, with her face tilted up and the skirt of her dress swaying in the breeze.

I tapped her on the shoulder. On bad days, when she was exhausted, I only saw my fingertips touching her.

On good days, I also physically felt it.

This wasn't one of them. We had to go home.

Cleo weaved her way around Adriana, purring and touching her ankles like a feline battery charger.

In the meantime, I prepared a cappuccino with a thick layer of milk foam and chocolate sprinkles. My relative had a fondness for the foam that almost rivaled her enthusiasm for champagne and wine.

Our little tabby purred louder and sped up her circling.

"Thank you, sweetie." Adriana blew her a kiss and Cleo jumped onto the sofa for a well-deserved nap.

Adriana dipped her finger into the milk foam. A droplet glistened on it, and she licked it off.

I relaxed. One or two drops were all she could take in on the best of days. I had no idea how much that equaled in ghost terms, but I knew that Cleo's recharging act had worked.

My great-great-aunt had recovered to sparkling form. She flung herself into the sofa, next to the sleepy kitty. "Don't you want to ask me something?"

I sipped my hot drink.

Cleo opened one eye and stared at me.

I dropped a spoonful of milk foam onto a saucer for her and put it on the floor.

She stared harder.

"If you want it, you have to come here," I said to her.

The furry little head swiveled from Adriana to me and the saucer and back to her spectral friend.

I took pity on Cleo and held the saucer so she could lap up her share without having to move too much.

"I'm listening," I told my great-great-aunt.

"The police know how Pierre was murdered," Adriana said. "Tilda had just received the autopsy report." She paused, for dramatic effect, and admired her almond-shaped nails.

I felt the blood drain from my face. I'd accepted that my old friend was gone. What I didn't want to discover was if he had suffered.

"He wouldn't have felt a thing," Adriana said as if she'd read my mind. "Really. And who knows, maybe we'll see him again, soon."

Considering that she hated to be reminded of the fact that she had left the official land of the living long before I'd been born, she'd given Pierre's demise a lot of thought. "I hope not," I said.

Adriana might have been living her best life in the here and now, with me and Cleo.

Picturing Pierre letting his hair down as a ghost though took more imagination than I had. The idea that every person whose life had been cut short by foul play in Cobblewood Cove might be hanging around had already given me nightmares when Adriana had turned up.

I could deal with having her by my side. The thought of dealing with a whole parade of not-too-dead folks on the other hand gave me the heebie-jeebies.

"That's mean." She pondered. "Unless Pierre isn't keen."

"Anyway, what did your investigative skills uncover?" I had to admit a tiny bit of curiosity. So what if I'd decided to leave the cops to do their job and not meddle even a little? It was only normal in my situation to wonder as much about the why as the who.

"Somebody used a bean-shooter." She formed a pistol with her hand and fired twice. "Instant death."

That explained the blood stains I'd noticed.

"Here's the interesting part." She blew the imaginary smoke off her gun.

"Don't tell me he did it himself because I'm not buying that."

"Applesauce. Of course, he didn't top himself. No, the cops think the thug had to shoot Pierre because the plan had gone all haywire. His booze was laced with sleeping pills, only he didn't drink any that night. What are you saying now?"

I mulled this over. "Then the killer must have broken in twice, right? First, to put the stuff into Pierre's drink, and then, when they expected him to be in dreamland."

"That's what our lady copper told her partner."

"That's a lot of risk," I said. "And for what exactly? I saw the open safe, but there must have been more missing."

She shrugged her shoulders. "I could break into the police station if you take me there."

"No. We're staying out of this." I had my reasons, apart from my decision to leave well alone. Adriana might be able to get into Fort Knox if I and her precious brick stayed close by, but there was no way she'd have the strength to break into closed drawers and rifle through case files.

Cleo yawned.

"Excuse me?" Adriana admonished her. "Let me finish."

The cat put a paw over her eyes.

"That's better." Adriana ran a finger over Cleo's spine. A blissful chirp rewarded her.

An alarm pinged on my phone. "You're in charge until I return," I told Adriana.

"You're leaving me?"

"Only for an hour or two. I've got a new movie for you." I dangled *I'm No Angel* in front of her.

"Mae West!" Adriana's voice took on a husky timbre. "Now that's some helluva broad. I saw her on Broadway, in that play that landed her in the cooler."

"It's got Cary Grant in it as well." I popped the DVD into the player and stole out of the room.

For the run time of the movie, my great-great-aunt would stay put.

She'd have a lot more fun than me, I thought on my way to the library.

The committee for the Cobblewood Cove culinary and craft festival, where I was headed, had formed in late spring, and the program had been sorted for weeks - until Pierre's murder.

His tastebud tickling treats (yes, that was going to be the official name of his contribution - the alliterations proliferated like dandelion in summer) had been the planned highlight at the opening and the grand finale, when artisans and chefs would receive best in show awards from discerning judges.

I only played a minor part as a gelato seller at the fair and as the designated minute taker for the committee. Nevertheless, duty called.

"Genie! You poor thing." Soft arms enveloped me, and the scent of an expensive perfume filled my nose.

Primrose Schuyler, who ran the show together with her sister, had a tear in her eye as she let go. "We very much wanted to check on you, after your ordeal, but then we weren't sure." Her voice trailed off. Both Schuyler sisters had aged since I saw them on our girls' night out.

They'd known Pierre all their lives. If it had been hard for me to deal with his death, it must be doubly hard for them.

Primrose took her place at the round table, next to her sister.

Fred filled a glass of water for her.

A 40-something stranger next to him rose to offer me his hand. He had a firm grip and an open face, with pearly white teeth and a chiseled chin. His bumpy nose, which must have been broken once, made him ruggedly handsome.

"You haven't met Genie Darling yet," Daphne said. "Genie, this is Grayson Butler, Pierre's nephew."

"I wish we could have met under better circumstances," he said.

"So do I." I took a closer look at him. He'd rolled up the sleeves of his suit jacket. Underneath, he wore a blue shirt. Something about him seemed familiar. It would come to me, in good time.

I readied myself with my notepad.

When we started out, I'd been foolish enough to record the meetings and afterward transcribe the notes. After wasting hours on such interesting side topics of obtaining weather forecasts months in advance, or the possibility of demanding matching marquees and decorations from all the prospective stallholders, and the importance of having the flower beds around the square replanted to show a dazzling display of plants in full bloom, I'd decided to save myself a lot of trouble. I only included the things I deemed necessary, or at least realistic.

Today, nobody had said a word after the greetings.

That is, until now. I'd been too busy trying to place the nephew to notice two women standing at the door, one blonde, one with black hair.

Katie and Olivia had dropped by. Katie nudged Olivia Goodge into the room.

In turn, Olivia said to her, "If there's anything you need me for, call me."

Katie nodded and tiptoed away, as befitted anyone using a public library.

"What's that about?" I whispered in Fred's ear.

"Katie Johnson's not one to mingle too much."

That was an understatement. Within six weeks of her arrival in Cobblewood Cove, everybody knew Olivia.

The only things I knew about Katie were, that she was partner with the Goodges, that she and Tammy appeared to be pals, and that she'd had an argument with Pierre in the day when he'd been upset about the break-in.

Olivia's chair scraped over the floor. The noise set my teeth on edge.

"Thank you to Primrose and Dahlia for inviting me to fill the empty seat on the committee," she said. "I'm sure the dear departed would have wanted us to go on as planned."

Daphne and I shared an eye-roll. There had been no love lost between any of the newcomers and Pierre, and he would have been the first to point it out.

"What do you think?" Daphne asked Grayson Butler. "Are you okay with Steve taking over from your uncle at the fair?"

"That's a mighty pair of boots to fill," Fred murmured.

"I certainly hope so," Grayson said. "I'll put it to him."

"What are your plans for the future?" Olivia asked in a sweet voice. "Are you going to step into your uncle's role?"

I hid my grin behind the notepad. She hadn't taken long to seize the heir up as her main competition.

"I'm more at home mixing bran mash," he said. "You don't have to worry about me taking over. That's not going to happen."

The cogs in my brain whirred and clicked into place. I'd figured out where I'd encountered Grayson before.

No wonder I'd been unable to identify his face, because I'd only heard his voice, trying to convince his uncle to sell *Butler's Pantry*.

Chapter Eight

Half an hour later the committee had decided to keep the current program in place for the festival week. The only question mark hung over Pierre's stall.

We were all shuffling to our feet when Olivia raised her hand for one final question.

Ever dutiful, I flipped my notepad open again.

"Is Steve going to use Pierre's old recipes?" she asked.

Grayson paused. "You'd have to ask him. Why?"

"I'm only curious, that's all." Her smile exposed all of her teeth and stopped short of her eyes.

Primrose banged, or rather tapped, the table with a gavel.

I shut my notepad. The meeting was over.

"That was a waste of time," I complained to my mother as soon as I'd softly closed the front door behind me.

Mae West should be good for another ten minutes or so and I appreciated the chance to have an uninterrupted mother-and-daughter chat.

Aimée arranged roses in a vase. She gave them a critical glance. "People need reassurance. They want to feel safe in the knowledge that things will go back to how they were."

"With one minor adjustment. No more Pierre." A bitter tone crept into my voice.

"Not everyone was as close to him as you and the Schuylers." She pulled out one rose and shortened the stem another half inch.

"It's all a nightmare. I didn't exactly expect tears, but the nephew showed as much emotion as a store window mannequin, and Olivia would love to be rid of the competition. At least it seemed like it."

"That's ridiculous." Aimée declared herself satisfied with her vase and put it on the mantel. "She's got a nice niche where Pierre didn't bother to go, with her clam chowder and cornbread and pizza."

"True."

"As for the nephew, we all grieve differently. Didn't you say he's a vet? A man who's used to seeing animals die will have his own way to deal with stuff."

"Also true. It's only -"

"That was a lulu!" A slender leg covered by silk stockings poked through the door, followed by the rest of Adriana. She did a quick shimmy before she buried her nose in the roses. "I think we should have a theme party when the girls come over next." She changed her pitch to a seductive tone that would have filled Mae West's heart with pride. "When I'm good, I'm very good." Adriana raked me over with her eyes. "But when I'm bad, I'm better."

"I'll leave you to your decorating," I told my mother before Adriana decided to reenact the whole movie for me.

"Take the magazine. I've marked the interesting pages for you." Aimée handed me a glossy publication.

Adriana ogled it. "Is that the one everyone in town is reading?"

I waited with my answer until we were safely upstairs and out of my mother's hearing. "How would I know?" I flicked through the pages. Travel features about upscale hotels in Europe and the Caribbean, a spread about the ten best ways to have an intimate wedding for less, and a food section with a dog-eared page did nothing to enlighten me.

The cover did ring a bell though. "Katie left a copy after her discussion with Pierre, and Olivia also had a copy," I said.

"She sure did." Adriana gave me a wide grin. "And so did dear little Tammy."

"It figures. She's the type who'd devour anything she thinks of as classy."

"She and Steve had a tiff about it." She smoothed her dress and left her remark dangling in the air, like a tasty bait just waiting for me to bite.

She had a surprise coming. I was not even remotely interested in other's people private affairs. Only daughterly courtesy led me to pick up the publication and take a peek at the article Aimée thought was interesting.

It didn't tell me much new, though. A cooking competition, publicized widely and with the winner due to become the cover star for the Christmas edition of the magazine, didn't fall under my definition of hot news.

If Olivia wanted to go for it, good on her. The one thing it did explain was her interest in Steve's access to the cherished recipes that had turned Pierre's into a legacy affair.

He'd kept the original leather-bound ledger in his safe, but once, when I'd published my first blog post mentioning his creations, he'd allowed me a glimpse of pages with faded cursive handwriting and later, typewritten notes.

The safe! "I'll be back in a moment," I told Adriana and ran downstairs, to grab the stack of newspapers from the basket in the mud room.

Tony and Aimée believed in keeping local journalism well and alive and were loyal subscribers.

When they were away, I piled up the issues. Everything they'd already read would be put aside to be taken to a paper recycling station once a month. The papers covering Pierre's murder should therefore be at hand.

I was still at the bottom of the stairs when I heard my phone ring upstairs. I doubled my speed, praying that Adriana would resist accepting the call.

She could do that in a pinch, thanks to her connection to electromagnetic waves.

We'd also taught Cleo where to put a strategic claw on a phone screen, in an emergency.

This, whatever it was, did not fall into that category, and since the other party would be unable to hear my great-great-aunt, it would only hurt my reputation if I treated a caller with silence. At the eighth ringtone, I burst into the room.

"Hello?" Too late. I checked the caller ID before I returned the call.

Matt picked up with commendable swiftness. "Hello, Genie."

In the background, I heard traffic noise. "Where are you? When will you be back?" I asked.

"I just pulled in at Jolene's. She's asked if you could come to hers." He gave a rueful little chuckle. "Not quite how I'd planned the evening, but then you and I will have some privacy once she's calmed down."

That sounded urgent if the unflappable Jolene was worried about something.

"I'll be right over," I said and ended the call.

"No, you won't, not looking like something the cat dragged in." Adriana crossed her arms, daring me to defy her. "There's a lot of women dangling after a sheikh like Matt."

"I'm fine."

She snorted and pointed at the mirror.

I gave in. Brushing my hair and adding a slick of lipstick and a spritz of Chanel 5 satisfied her, as it should.

Considering that my choice of scent had been dictated completely by Adriana's needs - anything related to her original life worked wonders for her - she should be happy.

The only one less than cheery was poor Cleo. She disliked being alone for too long, and try as she might, my mother was no substitute for a fun-loving ghost.

I pointed that out to Adriana, who chose to turn a deaf ear to my arguments and Cleo's plaintive meows.

She wrapped herself in the spiritual versions of her shawl, put on her opera gloves, and smoothed her locks. "Get a wriggle on," she told me.

For someone who had all the time in the world, patience was a virtue she hadn't heard of.

Jolene lived in the newer part of town, halfway between the center and the cliff edge, where houses were just that and not villas, and backyards were meant for barbecues and workshops instead of greenhouses.

Matt opened the door and greeted me with the kind of smile that set my pulse racing and Adriana's heart aflutter.

I wished we could be alone. Heck, I'd insist on it, once we had taken care of whatever bothered Jolene. A woman had the right to a little bit of privacy with her boyfriend once in a while.

"I'm in the back," Jolene called out. She'd added a screened porch to her modest two-story home, where she could sit and work on something technical while watching the birds. Several feeders were placed strategically throughout her yard, taking care not to offer cats any purchase.

Her feline neighbors forgave her only because she offered them shelter and belly rubs, as well as fresh fish, according to Adriana. Jolene sat on her porch, with her hands idle in her lap and her shoulders slumped. I'd never seen her like this.

Matt gave me a grim little nod. He too appeared worried about his cousin. "I'll make coffee," he said.

"I'll help." Adriana strutted in front of him, with her hips swaying in a clear imitation of Mae West. What my great-great-aunt lacked in curves compared to the late great mistress of the single entendre, she made up for in vivacity.

Jolene waited until Matt had rejoined us with hot beverages and cookies.

Adriana ogled him with proprietary fondness. "He is the bee's knees."

I sent out disapproving vibes. She had promised to keep her commentary to herself unless she had something vital to contribute. Admiring Matt did not meet that requirement, even if I agreed.

My great-great-aunt draped herself over a chair.

"What's wrong?" I asked Jolene after she'd stirred her coffee enough to make it splash.

"The lab report came back about the pills in Pierre's booze," she said.

"How do you - of course, Hank." One day his heart-to-hearts with his cousin and who knew who else would land him in deep trouble.

"I heard him talk to Tilda while I fixed the heat pump in the office next door."

Adriana winked at me. "That's our girl."

I winked back, only to have Matt stare at me. I blinked and wiped my eye. "A stray lash," I said, mentally both cheering for Officer Newby because there was still hope for his career after all if Jolene had snooped, and face-palming because of my lame excuse. "What did they say?"

Jolene's shoulders sagged even further. "It's the same sleeping pills Felix uses. They're prescription only."

"Who is Felix?" Matt asked.

"He's the man behind *Vine and Vinyl*," I explained. "And he's a friend of Jolene's."

A quick smile flashed over Matt's face.

"It's not like that," Jolene muttered. "I just don't want an innocent man to be accused. He'd be toast in this town."

"It's a long shot to jump from one brand of pill to seeing him behind prison bars. There must be hundreds of folks in Cobblewood Cove who take sleeping aids," I said. "What motive should he have to murder Pierre?"

"It's crazy," she admitted. "But why else would Hank have mentioned Felix at all to his partner?"

"That's true." Now I stirred my coffee, faster and faster, to help my thinking.

"What do the flatfeet think why Pierre was bumped off?" Adriana sat upright.

"Did Hank mention anything about a suspected motive?" I asked.

"All they have is the empty safe." Jolene took a sip of her beverage and grimaced when it burned her mouth.

"Do we have any clue what was inside?" Matt chimed in.

Despite my sadness for Pierre, I grinned to myself. My boyfriend had definitely caught the sleuthing bug.

Could ghosts rub off on people without the poor saps having any idea?

"Only a few mementos, the recipe book, and one thousand dollars in cash," Jolene said.

"That's all?" Matt blew out his breath.

"But what if our murderer didn't know that? What if they thought Pierre had a small fortune stashed away? Everybody knows he owned a prospering business, and he rarely spent money." The idea sounded plausible to me. I addressed Jolene. "Maybe you should mention that to your cousin."

"I will." Jolene squared her shoulders. "And I might have a chat with the doctor about my trouble sleeping."

It took me a moment to catch on. "You want to find out if he'd prescribe you the same medication as Felix."

We high-fived.

For an instant, Adriana's gloved hand touched mine as she joined in. She winked at me again.

I responded with a smile.

"This Felix guy," Matt said, with a studied casualness that would fool only a man. "Should I check him out for you?"

Adriana tickled his chin, the way she had done with Tammy. "We could go on the razzle, all of us."

Jolene glowered at Matt. He was related to her on her mother's side, while Hank belonged to her stepfather's family tree. If all the far-flung family members met up, they'd fill city hall.

For an only child like me, with few blood relatives around, present company excluded, it amazed me how she managed to be on close terms with every single one. But then Jolene was a people person, and she had the added advantage of being useful too, as an all-round handywoman.

"My offer stands," he said. "Or if you'd rather stay home and worry, I could take Genie along to meet the guy."

"Now we're cooking with gas." Adriana arched her delicate brows at me. "Once we got you dolled up good."

"Stop acting as if I've got a crush on Felix," Jolene said. "I don't, okay? I only happen to like him as a friend and potential business opportunity."

"I didn't mean to step onto your toes," Matt said. "I only thought, if I take a look at him I'd be able to tell you my gut feeling about him."

Jolene rolled her eyes at her cousin. "Right. You'll use your x-ray vision to peek into his head and figure out if he's a killer I let loose on the town."

"Stop it, you two," I said before those two got into a spat. "For what it's worth, I can't imagine him trying to poison Pierre, or shooting him in cold blood."

"Most killers don't come with a tattooed sign on their forehead," Matt said. "We both know that."

Adriana huffed. "We happen to be the smoothest operatives anywhere. You might remind your fella of Italy."

The corners of my mouth twitched. If Adriana criticized Matt, she must be seriously feeling slighted. Of course, she was right. Without Genie and Adriana Darling, there might still be two unsolved murder cases in Tuscany.

"I suppose it can't hurt, but only if you don't pester Felix," Jolene grudgingly said to Matt.

"She is carrying a torch for the piano man," Adriana said.

I agreed with her, although why should Jolene deny it, unless deep down, she doubted if Felix's hands were clean after all?

It'd be interesting to discover was the public opinion. After all, there was only one topic in Cobblewood Cove. People loved to speculate at any rate, even more so after a drink or two.

We should be able to collect a lot of information if I could keep my partner-in-crime away from sticking her pretty nose into other folk's drinks.

Chapter Nine

Vine and Vinyl looked nothing like I'd remembered it. For one thing, instead of playing his baby grand, Felix was busy chatting to Fred Ward about rare pressings and collectors' items.

Also, the wine part had been moved to *Foodstock*. At least the connecting door was open, so people could go back and forth.

Matt made a beeline for the shelf with the turntables. They must have been stowed elsewhere when Jolene took me here before, with good reason. Some of them were vintage and would have fetched a decent amount of money at an auction.

I had a shrewd idea why Fred hung around. As one of the stalwarts of the Cobblewood Cove museum (open Monday and Thursday afternoons and by appointment) and close friend of the Schuyler sisters, he might be after one of the vintage turntables for an exhibition.

A loan would be in their mutual interest, and Dahlia and Primrose might be inclined to believe that such a suggestion coming from a man would go down better. It could also be that the Schuylers simply didn't want to be beholden to Felix's sister, who after all had been at odds with their old friend Pierre.

With Jolene by my side and Adriana skipping ahead, I drifted over to the bar.

Olivia stood behind it. Her fingers drummed on the counter and her gaze flickered to the wall clock. "I can serve you one drink each before we close," she said.

Katie poked her head out of the office and retreated as she saw us.

I ordered a bottle of Californian Chardonnay for all of us to share and tried to casually listen in to the conversations around me.

"Makes you wonder why the police haven't booked anyone yet," one of the bridge club ladies said to her friend.

The friend moved closer and whispered, "I've been told they're waiting to bust a smuggling ring. Pierre had drugs in his apartment, I heard."

"Drugs?" The other gal noticed me and clammed up.

I gave Adriana a signal to take over the spying and stepped back.

Satisfied that I no longer counted, the bridge club lady moved closer to her confidante, and Adriana hopped onto an empty bar stool next to them. "You want me to tell you what these broads say?" she asked me. My great-great-aunt enjoyed herself.

I gave her a tiny nod.

"Drugs?" She repeated.

"Pills, and such. And alcohol. I've been told he had enough in his apartment to get this whole town drunk." Adriana's imitation caught the sanctimonious expression so well, that I would have laughed if the circumstances were different.

"You don't say," the second woman said, according to my fellow gumshoe.

One day I had to learn how to tell the bridge club members apart, but the whole gaggle could have been cloned. They all had the same blonde bob, the same dress sense, and the same botoxed smoothness to their faces that made their aging throats much more obvious.

"You could have knocked me over with a feather, I'm telling you."

"I don't know." Her friend pursed her lips and so did Adriana. "I mean, what do we really know about Pierre? A man of his age and never married." The woman's eyebrows rose the half inch they still could after all the injections. "And then all those spices he had. Who's to say what was really in the jars? Maybe that's how he had the drugs delivered. The spices must have covered up the smell so the sniffer dogs would be fooled."

Adriana rolled her eyes at me. "Give them five minutes, and they have him tied to Al Capone."

"You're awfully quiet," Jolene said as she took her seat next to me.

I'd sent her back to Matt and Fred with the wine.

"I'm just wondering why anyone would kill Pierre," I mused, loud enough to catch the ladies' attention.

Olivia gave a start. "Don't say that. I've heard it was a robbery gone wrong."

The bridge club ladies shared a knowing glance.

"Maybe they were after the cash in his safe," the first one, who was an inch taller than her friend, said.

"It's tempting fate to have a small fortune in your home," Olivia said.

"I wouldn't call what he had at hand a fortune," the bridge club lady said. "A couple of thousand is my understanding."

Olivia stared at her scanning device and the phone she took payments with. "That's a lot of cash these days."

"He was old-fashioned," the bridge club lady agreed. "People used to make jokes about it."

"He said you could trust electronics until you couldn't," Jolene said. "Having ready money at home isn't such a stupid move if you have deliveries to pay for. I never once knew him to have anything put in his tab, or to ask if he could pay later."

"Maybe if he'd done that, he'd still be here with us." Olivia clenched her hands. "I thought this town was perfect for us when we moved here. Now I'm not so sure."

"Where did you come from?" I asked.

"Oh, you know. Here and there."

Before I could ask her another question Olivia dashed out from behind the bar and signaled to her brother. "Closing time, folks."

"I thought we'd have a swell time on the town for a change," Adriana said. "We need to see some action." She wiggled one foot at me.

"Not now," I mouthed as I brought up the rear on our way out.

The bridge club ladies had beat Jolene and me by a minute or so. To my surprise, they were still in sight, loitering with intent until Fred came through the door.

I chuckled. As sweet as he was, I'd never thought of a bald, rotund man in his sixties as a lady's magnet. It appeared I'd been wrong.

Matt caught up with us, carrying a bottle of wine and a vinyl record in a bag. "What now?"

"Now we dissect our results. My place or yours?" I asked Jolene.

We filed around her kitchentable. The wine bottle stood untouched. Instead, we'd all decided on coffee. It would keep us alert, Adriana included.

She flitted around, inspecting her surroundings.

"Is it just me thinking this or was our evening a wash-out?" Jolene asked.

"I wouldn't say that," Matt said. "Your friend Felix checks out. He's a nice guy, and there's not a lot he can't tell you about old records and labels, down to the hardware." An excited gleam came into his eyes, one he usually reserved for me, in special moments. "He's got a lead on a Seeburg."

When this didn't ring a bell for any of us, he added, "They're considered to be the original jukebox makers.

They were way ahead of the game until the economy crashed and business dried up."

"Fascinating," Jolene said. "Except, what does that have to do with anything?"

I agreed. "Unless you believe that being an authority on his subject makes it impossible for Felix to have committed murder."

"It's a sidelight on his character." Matt showed us the recording he'd purchased, a pressing of Billie Holiday singing *I Can't Give You Anything But Love*. He gave me a slow smile that would have distracted me if we'd been alone. "I've heard you sing this so often, I had to snap it up for you."

"I told you he's the bee's knees." Adriana gave up her tour of Jolene's living room and came over to admire the record. I gave them both full marks for being right, only that the singing he'd heard tended to be a duet.

The screwball comedy *Bringing Up Baby*, where Katharine Hepburn and Cary Grant serenade a leopard with that song, had left a deep impression on Adriana, so we sang the song, a lot.

Matt showed us the spots where the vintage cardboard sleeve had been carefully repaired. "Any man who does such a painstaking job on an item he'll sell for less than 50 dollars, would do a much better job on planning a murder, apart from the lack of a motive."

Jolene gave him a questioning look.

"That's right," I said, mentally reproaching myself.

I'd found Pierre. I'd given the police the first witness statement. Yet I'd been too blind to do more than simply repeat facts. "Pierre's death has been sloppy."

Jolene's head jerked around.

So did Adriana's.

"There were sleeping pills found in the bottle, right?" I asked.

"That's what the report says." My great-great-aunt hopped onto the table and swung her legs. She said it helped her think.

"Then why was he shot?"

"He didn't have any of the laced drink and was awake when the killer broke in," Jolene said.

"Why bring a gun if you expect your victim to be knocked out or already dead?" I realized this question had been at the back of my mind for a while.

"As a backup plan?" Jolene groaned.

"Then why didn't I see any sign of a struggle? If a stranger breaks into your flat, you'd defend yourself. At least you'd reach for your phone." I screwed my eyes shut and pictured the scene. I'd found the body lying face-down on the floor. He must have been standing when the bullet pierced his flesh. He could have grabbed his phone from the coffee table, unless . . . "I think he trusted his killer, or he didn't hear him break in," I said.

Jolene gaped at me. "He wouldn't have known Felix well enough to trust him. But if he hadn't noticed a stranger entering, why not sneak away and wait a few more hours until Pierre had had his nightcap?"

"Good questions. I hope the police are asking them too, or figure out why Pierre had to die at all," Matt said. "Why not wait until he was at work or out for the night? You told me yourself you could set your clock by him. It would have been a lot easier to rob the place with him on the golf course or playing cards with the Schuylers."

"That's smart," Adriana said. "You should have thought of that, Genie."

"I did, just now." All eyes were on me. Blithely, I went on. "I just now felt a hunger pang. Should we order food, before I go all light-headed and ramble?"

"Chinese or Italian?" Jolene reached for her phone, pushing a magazine off the table in the process.

Weird. I'd never seen her be clumsy before. Something weighed on her mind, despite our best efforts to show that Felix had nothing to fear.

Matt pulled a face. So did Adriana. Either she'd tired of this less than exciting evening or she had news to share with only me.

I hesitated.

"Leave Matt to have a chin with Jolene," Adriana said. "She might be clamming up to you, but he'll crack open her shell like an oyster. Oh, that's good. Write it down."

When my cherished ancestor had that gleam in her eyes, I did as told.

While I secretly doubted that Adriana's pearls of wisdom would go down in the annals of history as great literature, I nevertheless kept notes. During her living, breathing days she'd dreamt of becoming the next

Dorothy Parker, and the mere obstacle of being officially dead would not stand in her way.

Also, she wasn't wrong. The question was, why would Jolene, who resembled not so much an open book but a whole billboard, be worried about Felix and reticent about the why at the same time?

I pretended I'd forgotten that I still had to whip up the next day's gelato, so I could leave her and Matt to have a heart-to-heart among family and toddle off, with my present in my hand.

"Don't play it yet," he said as we said a lingering good-bye at Jolene's door. "Old shellac records are easy to break, and you need the right equipment."

I promised to keep that in mind.

"This wasn't quite how I'd planned my return, especially since I'll have to be off again on another trip." Matt clasped my hands.

"Go on, give him a smooch." Adriana chuckled. She stood right behind him, picking a hair off his jacket. She studied it with a jaundiced eye before she let it drift to the floor. "It's all good, it's yours."

I gave Matt a hasty kiss. "Look after Jolene and come back soon."

Chapter Ten

I dropped onto the sofa, startling the cat.

Cleo fled to her faithful ally.

"She's hungry," Adriana told me. "And you interrupted her nap."

A lesser person would have pointed out the ample supply of dry and wet food in Cleo's bowls, but considering that they had been sitting there since this morning, I contained myself and dragged myself to the storage cupboard.

"I'm hungry too, Genie. And thirsty."

For someone not technically alive and needing sustenance, Adriana could be high maintenance. In most instances, her demands had a lot to do with boredom, or with a lack of energy. I bit back a cutting remark as I spotted her wan appearance.

Adriana at her best was all glowing, with dewy skin, sparkling eyes, and bright colors. Seeing her radiance dim, made my heart skip a beat.

What had happened?

I hurried to feed the cat and reheat a frozen beef bourguignon, the last of my supply of gourmet meals prepared by Pierre. While the microwave did its job, I wafted a spoonful of brandy under Adriana's nose.

Her natural glow returned.

"I should have left you at home," I said. "This whole running around and snooping is too much for you."

"Applesauce." She draped herself over the sofa. "One more noseful and I'll be all hotsy-totsy. Bring me your coat."

I gaped.

She snapped her fingers. "I slipped an object in your pocket. I've go to admit it was a little tricky." With this, she slipped deeper onto the sofa, and I wafted the brandy again.

My coat pockets held a clean tissue each, a few coins for donation boxes, and a folded piece of paper.

"That's the one," Adriana said with deep satisfaction.

I opened it and frowned. My great-great-aunt had gone to a lot of trouble to purloin the paper, but it beat me why. All I saw was a map for the festival week, with stalls centered around a gigantic tent where competitions and musical acts would form the main attractions.

"Look again," Adriana said when nothing came from me.

I did. It escaped me at first because I'd seen this map more often than I ever wanted during the early planning stages. I was about to give up when my gaze fell upon a change in the plan. The prime spot reserved for *Butler's Pantry* had been reallocated.

If Steve stepped in for Pierre, he'd do so at the edge of the square, close to the portable toilets. In his stead, the coveted position would now be taken over by Neely and Sallie Potts from the *Carrot Cove*, who'd share a booth with *Vine and Vinyl*. It showed remarkable tolerance on the Pottses side, considering that, vegetarian as grapes were, Felix's sister dealt in animal products.

My heart sank. Maybe we'd all been wrong and Felix had a motive after all, as ridiculous as it was to kill over the location of stalls at a festival that only ranked high in the minds of locals.

"Where did you find this?"

"On the floor. One of the old broads who was jawing off about drugs must have dropped it." She twinkled at me. "This just busted this case wide open."

Considering Jolene's closeness to Felix Goodge, it seemed wiser to ask someone else when the change in the layout had happened, and more importantly, why.

Pierre wasn't in his grave yet and already Cobblewood Cove's movers and shakers appeared to be moving on. Something about all this felt off.

Adriana gave me an expectant look. "Speechless?"

"Almost," I admitted.

"I told you I can pull off all sorts of stunts." She preened a little but deservedly so. Picking up a physical object that held no connection to herself, and depositing it in my pocket must have been the spectral equivalent of me bench-pressing a horse.

"What do we do next? Give Felix the third degree? Or maybe it's the vegetarian gals after all. Anyone who butchers the language with a name like *Carrot Cove* is capable of anything," Adriana said.

I envisaged the soulful owner of the vegetarian café and her mild-mannered daughter. I'd only seen them on a few occasions, yet I had a hard time picturing them as cold-blooded murderers, whatever they thought of people who made money selling meat. Plus, so far Pierre was the only victim. "I'm sure the police will be checking the Pottses out," I told my great-great-aunt.

She snorted. Her faith in the police was slightly underdeveloped, something I could understand. She'd grown up in an age when bribes flowed as easily as the moonshine which made the mob rich and the Roaring Twenties legendary.

"We can't sit on our behinds and do nothing. We owe it to Pierre. And if Jolene's beau has dirty hands, we've got to save her from herself," she said.

Cleo swished her tail in agreement.

"See that?" Adriana said. "Cleo thinks it's our duty. And she wants in on the action."

An inner alarm bell shrilled in my head. That Adriana considered herself the answer to Nancy Drew, I'd come to accept. That her feline sidekick had developed similar ambitions came as a surprise and not a welcome one. I could defend myself in sticky situations, and Adriana was already dead.

But an eight-pound tabby who'd lived a soft life ever since we'd adopted her, and who had needed a month

of coddling to recover from one fateful night when she
ventured outside and got chased by a seagull, was another matter. "How does she plan to do that?"

"Same as we do."

Cleo purred.

Adriana clasped my hand and closed her eyes. She
took a deep breath.

I let myself go limp. We'd done this before. It didn't
work for very long, and it exhausted Adriana, but she
could actually make me understand what Cleo said.

In this case, it was, "It's boring on my own."

"You can take a nap," I said.

Cleo cocked her head at me. "I can do things." She
unsheathed her claws and swiped at the air.

"There are dogs outside."

She yawned.

"And children. Lots and lots of small children, who'd
pat you and grab you and pull your tail."

Cleo jumped back, in apparent horror.

Adriana let go of me.

"We can share our information with you," I said to the
cat.

"Promise?" Adriana had taken over her translator duties again.

"Sure." After all, what harm was there in telling all to
a cat? It was humans you couldn't keep their lips zipped,
something I counted on for our next step, after a decent
rest period for all three of us.

"I swear I wonder what the world is coming to." Miss Lulu, owner and top stylist of *Goldilocks*, paused before she rinsed my hair. "I'm going to tell Jolene to put up new deadbolts around my house." Her voice trembled a little. Her hand, luckily for her clients, did not. Her mascara had smudged, as if she'd rubbed her eyes.

"I'm thinking of getting a guard dog," the little old lady sitting in the waiting area, or gossip central as Jolene had called it, said.

Since her remaining hair was sparse but immaculate, I assumed she visited Miss Lulu for the company.

"That's a mighty big responsibility," Miss Lulu said. "Food bills and the vet and all that. You could put up a warning sign and have one of those bells where you hear a bark when you ring. My sister-in-law down south has one of those contraptions."

"Is that right?" the old lady asked what had to be a rhetorical question.

"She says she sleeps like a baby, now she has that. And you don't have to walk a doorbell and clean up after it."

We all giggled at Miss Lulu's mild joke, although at least I struggled to do so.

She wrapped a towel around my hair. "Now, do you want a simple trim or try a different style?"

With the influx of new businesses and the prospect of the fair, many established shop owners had upped their game. For Miss Lulu, that included bringing her fashion into the 21st century at Formula 1 speed.

"A trim will do," I said. After all, I'd only come here for the information.

She stared blindly ahead. "That's exactly what Pierre said, only a week ago." Her lips wobbled. "I'm going to miss him."

"He would have put Cobblewood Cove on the map, mark my words," the little old lady said.

"Pierre didn't care about fame." Miss Lulu sectioned my hair and picked up her scissors. "There's been many occasions when people offered him a fortune for his recipes. He said to me, Lulu, some things are more important than being rich. I promised my dad to keep up our tradition, like he promised his dad before him, generation for generation."

"Still, it would have been lovely to see our town on TV," the little old lady said. "Now that chance is gone."

"Television?" I asked, confused.

"Well, he would have won that cooking contest with one hand tied to his back, if he'd been so inclined. And there was a bit in the papers and on the radio a while ago, that a film crew would come to record our local stars of the cousin, Pierre would have been a shoo-in."

It took a moment until the penny dropped. "Local cuisine, you mean?"

"That's what I said."

"There are still other contestants," Miss Lulu said. "Those new gals are pretty keen. And like I told you,

Pierre wasn't having any of this. He was happy enough staying in his own kitchen."

"There's nobody coming close to Pierre, and that's a fact, no matter what that Goodge woman and her partner think."

"What about the *Carrot Cove*?" I asked.

"That place where they only serve you boiled greens?" I watched in the mirror as the little old lady pressed her lips together. "The Pottses are nice enough women, but folks want a real meal on their plate."

"I heard that Pierre had planned to go away, on vacation." Miss Lulu compared two strands of my hair for length and nodded to herself. "He might still be around if he'd done that."

"He never mentioned anything to me," I said, bewildered. Had Pierre sensed that he was in danger?

"The whole town is going to miss him for sure," the little old lady said. "I only hope that the menu will stay the same."

"Not likely, is it? That man could work magic." Miss Lulu practically salivated.

The little old lady shrugged. "Recipes are recipes, that's what my gran used to say. All you have to do is follow them. No magic needed."

I fought back the urge to run out of the door when the importance of these words sank in.

Miss Lulu peered at me. "Anything wrong, honey? Only you need to sit still for me." She wielded her scissors.

"Probably cramps." The little old lady nodded to herself. "I had them something fierce when I was your age. They stopped right after I had my oldest."

I felt her gaze travel to my belly. Inwardly I groaned. I needed to get away before the words body clock were mentioned. The last thing I could tolerate was people speculating about my private affairs, or lack.

Styled and with more than enough food for thought, I left *Goldilocks*.

The next stop on my itinerary was the hardware store. Whereas I wasn't in the position to ask the police for information about the case, Officer Hank Newby would tell his dear cousin Jolene anything she wanted to know.

I had my hand on the door when another thought hit me. If the Goodges were involved, and Jolene planned to do business with Felix, sharing all my ideas and clues would be a bad idea. I had to get back to the drawing board.

CHAPTER ELEVEN

"There you are." Fred Ward waved at me. "I tried to call you."

"You did?" I checked my phone. It was off. I'd forgotten to recharge it. A cold shiver ran down my spine. What if Adriana had tried to reach me?

Fred, ever the gentleman, stepped between me and the road. "Pierre's lawyer has arrived, to tell you about his last will. She asked for you."

"She's not going to kick me out or double my rent?" I'd signed a contract of sorts with Pierre when I set up shop in *Butler's Pantry*, but I had no idea if it was legally binding. My old friend had always been as good as his word, so I'd never worried.

"I wouldn't know." Fred blinked.

"It's all a lot to take in." With a pang, I realized that he and Pierre had only been a few years apart.

I'd lost a surrogate godfather. Fred, and the Schuyler sisters, had lost a contemporary and with him, a part of their past.

I had no idea what to say, so I stayed silent until we reached the office at the city hall, where the lawyer had hung up her shingle for the day.

In the hallway, hardback chairs sat along the wall. Pierre's nephew was the only person waiting.

Fred knocked on the door.

A brisk woman in her fifties opened it and ushered us all in. While Pierre's lawyer shook hands, I took stock. Vera Polaski's five inch heels, which had surprised me at first, were probably intended less as fashion statements and more as a means to be taken seriously. Without them, she'd struggle to top five feet.

My friend Jilly used the same diminutive stature to great effect, when it came to appealing to chivalrous instincts. For a female law professional, the same helpless damsel ploy would be a hindrance.

"I'm very sorry about your loss," she said to Grayson.

His face clouded over. "Thank you."

"Shall we begin?"

"I'll wait outside," Fred said.

"That's not necessary." She opened a thin folder and prepared to read to us the last will of Tobias Peter Butler.

It gave me a jolt to hear Pierre's formal name. It made sense that all children of the family wouldn't be designated as the chosen Pierre at birth but be given a name that could be easily adjusted. I wondered how the Butlers had dealt with female offspring. Or maybe they'd taken a page out of the pope's playbook, where the new head of the church chose a new name. Didn't the British Royal family did the same thing?

A few words penetrated my mental babbling. " ... entire goes to my nephew, Grayson Peter Butler. However, I leave the sole right to decide over all business matters pertaining to *Butler's Pantry* and the associated building to Geneviève Darling Hepner who shall also be allowed to continue with her own business on said premises, rent-free, for as long as she wishes." Vera Polaski leaned back. "That's all from my side."

I stared at her. I was to make the business decisions?

Part of me wanted to decline. Except, this was what Pierre had wanted. How could I say no? I gave Grayson a sideward glance.

He looked as stunned as I felt. He caught up with me in the hallway, while the lawyer packed her bags.

"We need to talk," he said.

"We do."

His phone beeped. He checked it and groaned. "There's an emergency at my clinic. I don't know how long it will take. Can I come and see you later?"

"That's fine," I said.

Only when he rushed off did it dawn on me that he hadn't asked for my number.

Chapter Twelve

"We're in charge?" Adriana quirked an eyebrow. "Sort of."

We shared a grimace. Flattering as it was that Pierre had trusted me with the decision-making for what was as close to a venerated institution as Cobblewood Cove had to offer, I felt queasy.

Adriana echoed my unspoken thoughts. "Then we have to make sure we don't screw it up. We need to figure out who offed our friend before we let the wrong guys get their hands on his legacy."

"That's what's been bothering me," I said. "That's why I asked Jolene over."

"I thought you didn't want to involve her, in case the dude she's sweet on is a bad apple."

"I've changed my mind. She needs to know if she can trust Felix, even if it's only about a business connection for her. She's our friend, we can't keep her out of the loop."

While we waited for Jolene, or to hear from Grayson, we went over everything that we'd figured out so far. We ended up with more questions than answers.

One thing I was thankful for was that my mother was out of town for the night. The quieter I could keep my involvement in the case, the safer for everyone.

That was, if Adriana and I could narrow down the why with Jolene's help. Then she only had to feed our intel to her cousin, and the police could take over the rest.

Adriana pulled a face when I mentioned my reasoning.

Cleo twitched her ears in a manner that in a human would have been sarcastic.

I glared at the duo. "It's worth a shot, and I'd rather not stir up a killer. It should be enough to do our bit in the background."

Adriana patted my hand. It felt like a summer breeze touching my skin. "No one is a match for the derring-do Darling detectives, anywhere. We've proved that."

"We have. We've also had narrow escapes."

Cleo skittered over to Adriana. Because Adriana still touched me, I could hear the cat.

"I'll fight them all off." She growled and struck at the air.

"Thank you, that's very kind," I said.

"See?" Adriana broke physical contact, and Cleo's voice in my head changed into a normal meow. "Cleo and I will protect you."

Jolene sprinted up the staircase after I'd buzzed her in on the system she'd installed. Since she'd done most of the improvements to the house, I could rely on her to tread carefully on the one worn step instead of slipping on it. Still, I'd have preferred her holding onto the railing.

"You won't believe it," she exclaimed.

Adriana, who stood beside me, rubbed her hands.

"Tell us, I mean, me." I'd prepared a few snacks, which only served to remind me of my loss. In happier days, I'd have brought roast beef sandwiches and salads home from *Butler's Pantry*. Now, I couldn't even say if the establishment would exist much longer.

Jolene sank onto a chair and ogled the food.

"Have a bite," I said.

She chewed slowly and with all signs of appreciation, to my relief and Adriana's dismay.

My great-great-aunt loved food. Yet since all she could do was dine off the scents and at the very best, eat one morsel, if that's what she did with it, she struggled with understanding how much time we mortals could spend with eating. She rested on the sofa, with a purring Cleo by her side.

"I've heard gratulations are in order," Jolene said.

I looked at her in confusion.

"You're the chosen one, who wields all the power over Pierre's legacy? The only thing people can't decide on is if you also inherit a share of the business." She paused for a beat. "And a few idiots think it gives you a motive."

"Me?"

Adriana jumped up so fast that she startled the cat. "Who says that?"

I waved my hand behind my back, trying to tell her to relax.

"I don't inherit anything," I said. "I'd appreciate it if you would make that clear to whoever needs telling. But you were going to say something else."

"Right. I went to see the doctor and spun him a story about sleeping problems."

"What did he say?" I asked.

"He gave me a prescription, for the same pills Felix used, and the same pills discovered in Pierre's brandy." A broad grin spread over her face. "He says they're his go-to choice when it comes to sleeping aids, and Pierre had some himself - a bottle he'd asked for last year, for his nephew."

"That's strange. Why would Pierre ask for Grayson? He must have his own doctor."

"I don't know. But Pierre and he go back a long way, so he trusted him."

"That means a lot of people had access to those pills," I said.

"It certainly seems that way."

"Has your cousin told you anything else about the case?"

"Like what?"

"Like, have the police found Pierre's recipe book? He kept it in his safe."

"You mean that's what the murderer came for?"

"It's a possibility." I took my notepad where I had jotted down everything Adriana and I had thought of. "Depending on the motive, we have different suspects."

"There's the ledger," Adriana prompted me when my dramatic pause, while I took a sip of water, lasted too long for her liking.

"The ledger," I repeated. "It contained all those precious recipes collected over generations. Pierre never shared them with anyone, and he was offered lots of money to part with the secrets."

"I heard a few stories," Jolene said. "I'll check with my cousin." She quickly typed a message to Hank Newby. "Who's the suspect in that case? And what other motives do we have?"

"If Pierre was killed for the inheritance, the money's on the nephew. If he died to get rid of competition, it could be the Goodges or at a very long shot, the vegetarian women."

"Don't forget Steve," Adriana said. She rubbed her temple.

"Steve?" I stared at her.

"Genie?" Jolene waved a hand in front of my face. "Are you okay?"

"Sorry." I'd decided that my little missteps in dealing with a ghost were less obvious if I stopped explaining them away. "What do we know about Steve?"

"That he's a nice guy with really dubious taste in women." Jolene grinned. "We went to high school together. I took woodwork, he did cooking classes, and if he had anything to do with Pierre's death, I'll eat my hard hat."

Since she hadn't so much as blinked when I mentioned the Goodges, she either was convinced of their innocence or she wilfully ignored the possibility. Granted, I had trouble picturing a sensitive musician or his sister murdering Pierre to increase their business success rate, but people had committed crimes for less motive.

But of course, the likeliest candidate was the nephew, who took this moment to announce his arrival. Or rather, to my surprise he had Daphne announce him in a phone call.

Since Cleo showed off her claws and her incisors, I thought it more prudent to suggest meeting him at Daphne's. After all, if he'd already arrived at our librarian friend's place, we might as well go there.

Cleo protested a little when she saw me grab my coat and Adriana hold the spiritual copy of her vanity case, which increased her spectral life force.

"We'll soon be back," I promised. "You don't like too many strangers around."

"Especially if they smell of vet practice." Jolene stroked Cleo's head.

Cleo gave Adriana a pleading glance. My great-great-aunt whispered something into the furry ear. "We're ready," she told me.

Jolene shook her head. "I'll never understand cats. I'm one hundred percent sure Cleo likes me and she loves being stroked, but she's constantly staring at something I can't see."

Or someone, I thought. "She does that with everyone," I said. "She probably wants to keep up the feline mystique."

Chuckling, we closed the door behind us, to stroll towards the town center and Daphne's place.

Chapter Thirteen

Fine lines crisscrossed Grayson's forehead. He looked exhausted.

Adriana gave him the once-over when he left his spot by Daphne's fake fireplace to greet us.

Jolene half-turned to me before she shook his hand.

I concentrated on my librarian friend.

She watched Grayson with the kind of worried gaze reserved for children, or loved ones.

I suppressed a groan. The last thing we needed was another romantic entanglement. They only lead to complications.

"It's good of you to come," Grayson told me. "And your friend."

"It's no hardship." Jolene treated him to a big grin. "Can't miss a chance to visit with Daphne."

We settled around the living room table. A soft moan came from a spot behind the sofa.

Jolene and I both flinched until I heard Adriana giggle.

"It's only a dog," she told me.

Daphne's face lit up. "You haven't met my new family member yet." She crouched behind the sofa and returned with a grey-haired dog of indeterminate breed.

He wheezed a little.

"Toto's a hospice dog. Grayson got him for me." She sounded besotted, although I couldn't say with whom of the two.

"That's partly what I wanted to talk to you about," Grayson said to me.

"Hospice dogs?" He had me confused. "I love animals, but I'm not sure our cat would be happy."

"Of course she would." Adriana's gaze became misty. "Say that we can adopt a few dogs. I can take them for walks."

"Later," I whispered.

Grayson smiled, and his worry lines smoothed. With a shock, I realized that he reminded me of Pierre. "We're only too happy to have people take in an old dog or cat."

Adriana nodded so enthusiastically that she lost her balance and fell off the arm of my chair onto the sofa, next to Daphne and the dog. Or maybe that had been her intention all along because Toto's wheeze changed into a blissful snuffle and he pressed his muzzle into her hand.

I turned my gaze away from ghost and dog, towards the heir. "I sense a but."

"What I need you to do is allow me to sell *Butler's Pantry*."

"Say that again." Jolene beat me to the very words.

Daphne gave me an apologetic shrug.

"It's the best solution," Grayson insisted. "There is nobody to take over the business." His voice held a hard edge. It sounded so much like his discussion with Pierre I'd overheard that I didn't trust myself to meet his gaze.

Instead, I stared at the floor and saw Grayson's shoes. He wore a pair of sneakers, and they also were familiar.

I got a jolt. Grayson had been the guy chatting with Steve behind the dumpster.

I forced myself to relax. Maybe there was an innocent explanation. Daphne clearly liked the guy, and he was Pierre's flesh and blood. "Can't that wait? Your uncle isn't even in his grave yet."

I watched his reaction from under my lashes, and so did Adriana.

"Why delay it?" he asked.

"I don't know, respect? Or to decide what possible options there are going forward? *Butler's Pantry* meant the world to your uncle. Don't you think it matters what he would have wanted?" I asked.

"In that case, he should have selected a successor and trained him." Grayson's voice rose.

Daphne touched his arm. "We're all a little on edge, so let's take a deep breath here."

"I need the money fast." Grayson's jaw muscles worked.

"No kidding," Adriana muttered.

"So urgently that a few days or weeks would make all the difference?" I asked.

Jolene whispered a few words into my ears.

They confirmed what I'd already guessed. I fixed Grayson with a hard stare. "Or do you think it'll affect the price if potential buyers hear that the treasure trove of original recipes is gone?"

His jaw dropped.

Jolene said, "The police haven't found any trace of the ledger."

"That's ridiculous," Grayson said.

Daphne frowned at him.

I felt a stab of pity for her if she indeed was fond of him. His words rang too hollow to be convincing. Any member of the family surely would have been in touch with the police about an heirloom that held the same importance for the Butlers as the brick nestling in my purse held for Adriana. They were at the core of their being.

"Why should the recipes have anything to do with the value of Pierre's business? The important parts were written in a code and was the only one able to decipher it. That knowledge died with him." He fixed me with an inscrutable stare. "Unless he shared that information with someone."

"Not with me, I assure you." But Grayson was right. When Pierre allowed me that small glimpse, back in the old days when my life was free from murders and ghosts, there'd been parts missing, or at least they hadn't been spelled out in plain English.

Adriana whispered, "Ask him if Pierre kept a code book, or if he'd memorized everything." She raised her voice. "Tell us, what are the 39 Steps?" She mimed going into a trance.

Maybe I should cut down on our classic movie sessions.

"Wouldn't he have written down the explanations somewhere safe?" Jolene asked. "I'm sure Pierre would have been too smart to risk that information being lost for good, if he had an accident or a stroke or something."

"That makes sense." Daphne moved a little closer to Grayson as if trying to protect him while siding with us. Divided loyalties could be a bummer.

"He did." Grayson shrugged his shoulders. "Except I have no idea where. I thought, maybe he kept his secret notebook with you, Genie."

"I'm not a Butler. What I don't understand is, why didn't he store his code book with you?"

"That's right," Adriana said. "I think he might be our guy after all. He had the pills, he had the motive, and he has killed before."

I gave her a perplexed look.

"He's a veterinarian, they have to put down animals all the time," she said.

Factually, I couldn't argue with that, although I was pretty sure that being able to end a pet's suffering was in a different league from killing your uncle for the heritage. I had another question, which I hoped Jolene would pass on to her cousin, the police officer. "Just because you were aware that Pierre had used a code . . ."

"Actually, that cipher had been handed down for a couple of generations," Grayson corrected me.

Daphne petted her dog who'd fallen asleep again. "I wonder which one they used. There are a few nifty tricks that have been used since Roman times." The awe in her voice told me that she'd spend her next days at work researching on her library computer if she didn't have the books she wanted already sitting in the non-fiction section.

"The question is, would the killer have been aware of that? Did you two have any idea the important parts of the recipe book were encrypted?"

Jolene and Daphne shrugged in unison. "I don't think anybody had a clue. There was no reason to know," Daphne said.

"Which means, Pierre and Steve were probably the only ones, apart from you." I nodded at Grayson.

"I think you can cross Steve off that list as well," Jolene said.

"That's right. He once told me that we should invite Pierre to be on our trivia quiz team because the old man had a memory like an elephant. He didn't ever write down notes, Steve said." The corners of Jolene's mouth turned down. "That was a few years ago, long before the precious fiancée came along, or Genie moved to town."

"So, he could have found out since then," I said.

"He might, but then I'd have heard about it. It's the kind of thing you'd have mentioned to friends, or at least it's what Steve would have done."

"Does that answer your question?" Grayson asked me. "If you're worried about your own business, I can promise you that I'll honor my uncle's wishes. Whoever buys *Butler's Pantry* will have to let you stay rent-free."

I'd almost forgotten about that part of the will. I could sell our ice cream anywhere, as long as my great-great-aunt worked her particular magic. I'd think about that once I could be one hundred percent certain that our perpetrator would not profit from his crime. "You still haven't said why you're so keen on selling straight away." My heartbeat accelerated, despite my best efforts to keep calm.

At the back of my mind, I still heard Grayson and Pierre's heated words.

"It's not really a secret, is it? And you're among friends here," Daphne said.

"Famous last words." Adriana gave me a pointed look.

I answered with a little shrug, only to remember too late that for everyone else, she was invisible and I'd just shrugged at nobody at all. I moved a little so it appeared as if I'd meant Jolene, who winked at me.

"I have an offer. The buyers wanted me to talk to Pierre for them, but of course, he was too stubborn to listen." A tinge of sadness flickered over Grayson's face. "It still stands for a few more days. Afterward, the buyers will move on."

"And you need the money urgently?" Would a killer admit such a strong motive? Or maybe he thought that because he admitted it, we would take that as proof of his innocence.

"Yes. There's a building on the outskirts of Cobble-wood Cove that would be perfect for me. It already has a few kennels, enough land to build more, and the rooms are ideal." Grayson and Daphne's hands met over Toto's sleepy form.

"It's for a free clinic," she said. "One where old dogs and cats could also be cared for until they find a new home, and where people who are too broke to pay for a vet could come with their animals."

"That's a great cause," I said.

Adriana beamed at Daphne and Grayson.

He said, "That's what I tried to tell my uncle. He'd already had two heart attacks, for goodness' sake, he needed to retire. I'm not saying feeding people isn't im-portant. But seeing folks having to give up their dogs and cats when money is tight or they start to rack up veterinary care costs is heartbreaking. We could do so much good with the money from the inheritance."

We? Adriana and I exchanged a glance. Luckily she'd changed her seating position so this also included Jo-lene.

"I've volunteered to assist." Daphne blew her now snoring dog a kiss. "It'll be nice to have a change of scenery after work."

"I understand," I said. "Why don't you share the infor-mation about your potential buyers and their plans and we'll talk it over in a day or two?"

"I'd appreciate it." Grayson ruffled his hair. "I get that it might appear callous."

"No, I understand." I truly did. I also understood that his desire to help animals in need gave him a heck of a motive. It was hard to picture him killing his uncle just to put his hands on a pile of money.

But a man fired up with idealism might decide that the benefit of the many outweighed sacrificing one man.

Chapter Fourteen

W e said goodbye to Jolene on Daphne's doorstep. A stroll home in the crisp night air might help me clear my head. It also allowed Adriana and me to chat.

"I don't think the nephew bumped off Pierre," she said.

"That's because he's an animal lover, and it's tough to think bad of someone who takes care of them."

"I'm a great judge of character. He thinks so too." She crouched to pet one of the canine neighbors through the fence.

Dachshund Groucho pressed himself against the posts and yapped.

"That still doesn't explain why he avoided mentioning his little secret tête-a-tête with Steve, not long before his uncle died," I said.

"What are you talking about?"

"I saw them, or at least, I saw his foot."

Groucho's owner called him inside, and Adriana tore herself away. She tapped her nose. "Interesting. What do you think it means?"

That was the rub. I had no idea, except that it seemed suspicious.

Back home, Adriana collapsed on the sofa, with her doting feline companion by her side, while I dished out the cat food.

Adriana lifted a slender leg to admire her dance shoe. "What a pity you don't wear these anymore. It must be such a drag to put on those weird rubber thingies that Groucho's owner wore."

I had to agree. Adriana's glamour was a far cry from sweatpants and modern shoes, although she did approve of jeans and my Doc Martens, which now sat on their rack in the hallway.

At the back of my mind, a tiny bit of information tried to get through to me. Alas, that would have to wait. I needed all my remaining powers of concentration to create our final batch of ice cream for the next few days.

Adriana took up her preferred chef pose, which meant she floated onto the kitchen table and let me wave a small bowl with fruit and spices under her nose.

We never had fixed formulas, but then our ingredients also changed. Even fruit rarely had the same sweetness or juiciness in different deliveries.

That attention to detail which only my dear ghost was capable of, was the secret of our success. It also meant that Adriana deservedly enjoyed her starring role.

The rest of the world, or at least Cobblewood Cove saw only me in connection with *Gems and Gelato*. The least I could do to make it up to the real brain behind the creamy confections was to let her decide what we were going to create and how to call it. Only our traditional flavors, like chocolate and cherry, had started with traditional names.

Pierre had been the first to encourage me to come up with monikers as original as our gelato. I blinked away a tear before it could roll down my cheek and drop into *Daredevil's Delight*, a combination of pears, with pepper and a hint of cardamom.

Adriana had named it after her mother. Apparently, my "Daredevil" ancestor had loved climbing a pear tree in the backyard with her daughter. We couldn't bring back Rosalind (at least I hoped so, as much as I would have liked to meet her), or the tree, but we could create the feeling for my spectral companion.

So far, her mom was the only family member she'd created a special ice cream for. I hoped that one day she'd be inspired by her younger brother, my direct forebear.

While the mixture churned, I lit a fire.

Cleo stretched out in front of the vintage fireguard.

Adriana put her hand on mine. "It'll be alright. If we have to, we'll put the screws on them all."

Cleo showed her incisors. "I'll give those thugs a taste of me."

I gaped at her. I'd become used to the fact that physical contact with Adriana allowed me to understand certain animals. Their words formed a kind of echo in my head.

What took me by surprise was Cleo's word choice. Had watching movies with us turned her into a mini-me of my great-great-aunt? Now they both cocked their heads at me, mirroring each other.

The morning dawned bright and clear, and Adriana did her best to smooth my weary brows.

She'd gone all out to nudge my slippers into place, so I only had to step into them. From the kitchenette came the enticing aroma of fresh coffee.

"Thanks." I used the frother to create enough milk foam for the cat, the ghost, and myself.

Adriana had learned how to switch on the coffee machine using her power over electricity, so all I had to do was fill in water and coffee powder the night before. She bustled around, like a flapper version of a 1950s TV housewife. "Is everything peachy?" She battered her long lashes at me.

"Perfect," I told her. I filled Cleo's saucer with a bit of milk foam and held out the spoon for Adriana.

She stripped off her evening gloves and dipped her fingertip into the milk. "What are we going to do next?" she asked.

"Figure out who the prospective buyers are." I'd thought about it before I went to sleep. It might seem farfetched to think that a stranger would have Pierre bumped off for his property, when there were thousands of diners and restaurants for sale, in a thousand small towns similar to ours. Yet due diligence demanded we put them on our suspect list.

Grayson had emailed me a few pages with their details and offers.

Adriana read over my shoulder while I enjoyed my second cup of coffee and a slice of toast with jam.

It all appeared genuine to me. A group of investors, who owned various non-chain eateries across the Eastern seaboard and were attracted by the history of stellar reputation of *Butler's Pantry* - so far, so good. Except for one question.

Adriana beat me to it. "Why would they knock on the nephew's door while Pierre was alive?"

"That's one thing I intend to ask Grayson." Hopefully, Matt could cover the other side of the investigation, namely telling me if these investors were for real. As a museum security and insurance expert he knew enough people who moved in those kinds of circles.

I almost sent him a message, when I had an even better idea. Instead of asking my boyfriend to nose around and potentially delay his return, I could make use of a source closer to home.

Today my mother and her husband were due to return fresh from the Big Apple, and as a wealthy, well-connected entrepreneur and philanthropist, Tony was ideally suited to discover what was going on behind the scenes.

Adriana agreed. "It's much better if we keep the investigation under control. We don't want Matt to step on the wrong toes, without being around to save him. If you want to keep up with the Darling detectives you have big galoshes to fill."

"Galoshes." I felt a shot of excitement surge through my veins. I scrolled through my messages, including pictures Jilly had taken of her foot encased in a gigantic plastic boot. She'd written, *"Heard about Pierre. Too, too horrible. Say the word and we'll come running, or at in my case, hobbling. I borrowed three pairs of socks and hiking boots, and they still didn't fit, so I fell. No need to worry – It's only a sprain, and I've got a pair of crutches."*

I'd only glimpsed at her missives, after telling her to stay put and not to worry. "That's it." I showed Adriana the message. "That's what's been bothering me."

Ghost and cat both frowned, a facial expression only a person trained by my great-great-aunt would have spotted on the furry face of our little tabby. I was fast becoming an expert in many areas, I thought with a little well-deserved smugness.

Not included in my talents, sadly, were simple arithmetics, like putting two and two together when the facts were right under my nose.

Adriana drummed her fingertips on the table.

Cleo flicked her tail.

Both actions meant the same thing. Their patience with me was growing thin.

"One moment," I said and rang Jolene.

She picked up out of breath. "Hey, Genie."

"Am I disturbing you?"

She laughed. "Of course not. What can I do for you?"

I heard a faint male voice in the background. "Who's there? Felix?"

"He's having a problem with an old pipe. Why? Oh, I see. You don't want to be overheard."

I listened to her move around. "Okay, girlfriend. I'm all ears."

"I only have one question. There was a footprint in Pierre's apartment. Did your cousin mention that?"

Jolene lowered her voice. "He told me this morning. The police think it belongs to a man. I've looked at you-know-who's feet. They're too narrow, from what Hank told me."

"Be careful, anyway." I ended the call. "What do you remember about the night of the murder?" I asked my great-great-aunt.

Cleo's fur bristled.

Adriana shuddered. "Only that we had the worst weather in weeks."

"We did, but only for a couple of hours. Why then would our killer risk leaving a footprint when all they had to was wait until the downpour stopped? And a partial print means they either dried their soles not good enough or --" I paused.

"They planned to leave a clue!" Adriana pointed the tip of her shoe at me. "Only, why? I thought the flatfeet can tell the size and all that stuff with just one look."

"It's a bit more complicated than that. But in a nutshell, yes. Except, what if our murderer put on galoshes or wore three pairs of socks to make much bigger shoes fit? Then the police would follow the wrong trail."

"That's devious. Only we're smarter." She held her hand up for a high five, giving me a tingly sensation.

A tentative knock on the door interrupted us. "We're back," my mother called out.

"Come in," I said.

Adriana pouted. "We weren't finished yet."

I rolled my eyes at her as my mother entered.

Cleo waited for a sign from my great-great-aunt before she deigned to greet her official owner.

I suppressed a snicker.

This one-sided feline stand-off had been going on for weeks. Adriana had taken it to heart that Aimée Darling simply wouldn't catch on to our ancestor's presence at all, and my mother tended to be torn between feelings of guilt for leaving most of Cleo's care to me and instants of competitiveness.

"I thought you'd return tonight," I said to Aimée. "Would you like a hot beverage?"

"Tea would be lovely." My mother unwound a scarf she'd been wearing around her head, to protect her hair.

I took it and hung it on the coat stand.

A squeaking floorboard told me that Tony was joining us. He tapped on the open door.

I put down a second teacup for him.

"Are you in trouble?" he asked bluntly.

"What? Why?"

"Fred Ward called me about the will. There's a few people who wonder about what exactly your relationship with Pierre was."

Heat rose in my face. "I hope you told them to take their minds out of the gutter and show a bit of respect."

He chuckled. "No need. Fred's already taken care of that."

"He only wanted to warn us." My mom sipped her tea.

"That's kind. Unnecessary, but kind. There is something else you could do for me," I said.

"You only have to ask."

I handed Tony a piece of paper with the names of the investment company and their board of directors. "Can you discreetly make inquiries if they're serious about wanting to buy Pierre's building, and if so, why on earth they decided to use Grayson Butler as a go-between?"

Tony whistled through his teeth. "That is strange."

"That's what I thought. It's also possible that another person faked the offer." I must have sounded more worried than I'd thought, or Tony wouldn't have given me a swift hug. We got along great, but we both weren't compulsive huggers.

"Leave it all to us," my mother said.

"Please be careful to keep it all on the down-low," I said.

Tony said, "Give me a couple of hours and I'll have the goods for you."

"You'll be careful, though?" Aimée asked me.

Now it was my turn to hug my mom. "I promise. I only want to do what Pierre would have wanted me to."

"You will, sweetheart. Otherwise, he would have given the job to someone else."

I left the house in a more cheerful frame of mind, to deliver the ice cream to the *Cocoa Cabana*, while Tony did his bit of sleuthing. Adriana accompanied me, so my mother and Cleo had a few hours of uninterrupted bonding time. At least that's what I hoped.

My merry ghost settled on the passenger seat, where she could keep an eye on the stainless steel tubs once I'd adjusted her mirror.

"Wait," she called out as we were coming up to the green.

I squeezed my Toyota into a parking space in front of the library.

Adriana hopped out of the car.

I winced. I preferred if she waited until I'd opened the door. Watching her move through walls or in this case metal and glass, made my stomach churn. I followed her. "What is it?"

"Groucho's ball is stuck on a tree." She pointed at the newly designated doggy play area, where the dachshund barked at a ten foot chestnut, while his owner stood by, with a sheepish expression. "Sorry, buddy, I'll get you another toy," the woman told him.

Groucho barked again.

"I'll be back in two shakes of a lamb's tail," Adriana told me.

Groucho calmed down the instant he saw - or sensed - her.

I settled on a bench while my great-great-aunt floated in the air until she grabbed a sturdy branch and hauled herself up.

The tennis ball was caught between two branches.

Groucho stared wide-eyed, and so did I, as Adriana made a fist and punched his toy with all her might.

It moved a little.

She punched it again and again until it came free and fell to the ground, where Groucho pounced upon it.

"Did you see that?" Groucho's owner asked me.

"Pardon?"

"I could have sworn that darned thing was stuck for eternity."

"I didn't see anything," I lied.

She gazed at the tree, and her dog, and the tree again.

"The breeze might have shifted it." I felt good about that explanation. It made enough sense to stop the woman wondering all day. Those things were prone to start a headache otherwise. "You have an expressive throw," I said.

"Not me." She picked up a bright orange dog ball launcher. "It's this thing here. The woman at the *Carrot Cove* gave it to me."

"The vegetarian café?"

"That's the one. It makes you wonder what she'd want with a dog toy, doesn't it? Unless she feeds her pooch tofu." She chuckled.

I feigned a chortle, too.

Why was Adriana still sitting up in the tree? She should be down here with me, or letting herself be thanked by Groucho.

"Their food is pretty great," the woman told me. "If you ask me, they're in with a chance to win the competition, if they can get the right place at the fair."

"The right place?" I only half-listened.

The woman whistled for Groucho.

He came running, his precious ball in his mouth.

"You haven't been around for too long, honey. If you want to impress the judges, foot traffic is the way to do it. And you'll receive the most attention when you secure a table in the center. I've been involved in this kind of event planning longer than you've been alive, so, if you have intentions of making a name for yourself, that's what you should go for."

"I'll keep that in mind."

Finally, with a languid air, Adriana came down.

I hurried to meet her. Her hair had lost its sheen, but at least she hadn't become translucent yet. Saving that stupid ball had sapped her energy. I held the purse with her life-force-enhancing brick as close to her as possible.

She shivered a little.

"Stay still," I told her.

She swayed and grabbed my arm. "That's better."

I led her to the car and insisted on her waiting for me with the brick by her feet, while I dropped off the gelato tubs.

The refueling session had worked by the time I re-joined her. "That was a doozy," she said.

"The next time, how about you tell me what you're planning to do, so I can stay close? Or try to knock that stupid ball out of the tree myself?"

She kept quiet for a full minute. "You were worried."

"A little," I admitted. "What do you expect?"

"That's sweet of you." She leaned her head against my shoulder. If I closed my eyes, I could almost feel its weight. "It was worth it, though, wasn't it? To see Groucho happy? Or why did you have that little smirk on your face?" She pushed up the corners of her mouth with her fingers.

"I don't smirk, ever."

"Right."

"Let's just say we might want to have a chat with all the chefs in the competition. The Schuylers should be able to give me the full list," I said.

"I like the sound of that."

I started the car, only for the police to drive past.

In the back, I spotted Grayson Butler, a stunned expression on his face.

Daphne came dashing out of the library.

I honked, and she jerked my passenger door open. "They've arrested him."

CHAPTER FIFTEEN

Adriana and I hopped out of the car, with both of us using my side, so my great-great-aunt avoided contact with Daphne who still stood shell-shocked on the sidewalk.

"It's okay." I put my arm around Daphne's shoulders. "We'll go back inside, and then we'll talk."

Only a handful of customers watched us from the fiction aisle and the reading nook as we entered the library.

"Everything's fine," I said to the whole room.

Right on cue, people returned to their browsing, although I could already hear the wheels in their minds spinning with delicious speculations.

I craned my neck to see if Fred was on duty, but for once, Cobblewood Cove's Boy Friday must be on one of his other volunteer jobs.

That meant I had to leave the office door open. I'd hoped for total privacy but shock or no shock, Daphne had a reputation to uphold. Running out of the building without a substitute was already unheard of. If we now barricaded ourselves behind a closed door, Cobblewood Cove's tongues would wag until they had blisters.

I busied myself with putting Daphne's water jug to the boil. "Where's your tea and coffee?"

"No need for that," she said. A tiny smile flickered up as she unlocked a drawer and took out a flask and a glass. "Purely medicinal, of course," she said.

"Well, naturally."

She poured herself a small dose of brandy and downed it in one go.

Adriana's nose twitched. I shot her a warning glare, to stay away from the booze.

"What's going on?" I asked Daphne.

"Grayson came around to check on Toto."

At the sound of his name, a small head poked out from under the desk. Toto's nose touched the legs of my great-great-aunt, who sat on top.

"Hey, sweetie," she cooed. To me, she said, "He looks good to me."

"He had trouble eating this morning." Daphne fidgeted in her chair. "I've never had a hospice dog before, so I was a little anxious."

That earned her an emphatic nod from Adriana, and from me.

"You called Grayson?" I prompted her.

"He'd taken a few days off, what with the murder and everything, so he came here straight away." Daphne swallowed.

"What did he say?" Adriana scratched Toto behind his ears, and the tip of his tongue lolled out in bliss.

"He was writing me a list of food I should try when he received a call." Daphne's hand reached for the flask.

I whisked it out of her way. "You want to keep a clear head."

"Right. There he was, turning white as a sheet. It had something to do with his shoes, that much I could hear, and they wanted him for questioning."

"His shoes," I repeated.

"He left right away, and the police car was already waiting outside." She bit back tears. "I swear to you, Genie, he's innocent, and we have to prove it."

"Leave it to us," Adriana said. "We're so going to smoke out the thugs who did it."

Daphne clung to my arm. "Do you think Jolene will help?"

"Absolutely she will." I reached for my phone, to send her a message.

"Maybe I'll have one more drop," Daphne said.

"At least it's not poisoned, like Pierre's brandy." I handed her the flask when it hit me what I'd said. Now we really needed Jolene and her access to the police.

Before I could whip out my phone, an urgent knock on the open door startled us all. There, with perfect timing, stood the very woman I was just about to call.

Daphne exhaled. "Thank goodness it's you."

Jolene put down her toolbox and enveloped our friend in a hug. "I couldn't believe it when I heard that your boyfriend's been arrested."

Adriana and I shared a glance. So it was serious after all, or Jolene wouldn't have used the B-word.

"He wouldn't be the first in my dating history," Daphne attempted to quip, but I could see she was scared for Grayson.

"I don't believe it," Jolene said. "And neither does Genie."

I'd thought about it long and hard, and the brandy had clinched it for me. "I think he's been set up."

"Exactly," Jolene said.

"I also think we could prove it."

Daphne started at me as if I'd turned before her very eyes into Santa or at least one of his little helpers.

"We all were acquainted with Pierre's habits," I prompted.

"We were?" Daphne frowned. "I wasn't, except for his coming to the library and checking out two books for the weekend, every Friday, without fail. One historical fiction, one non-fiction."

"Well, I knew them, and I'm telling you that Pierre wouldn't have touched brandy on the weekend. On those days, he used to treat himself to a whisky sour, never more than one, and never after midnight." I waited for a reaction.

"And?" Daphne asked.

Adriana gave Daphne a pitying head shake as she danced around me. "She really isn't thinking straight," she told me.

I elaborated. "If I have all this information, how likely is it that his only nephew would be so clueless to lace the wrong bottle with sleeping pills? It's a nice tidbit to pass on to your cousin." I wiggled my brows at Jolene.

Since my great-great-aunt had perfected her one-eyebrow quirk, this would have to do for me. Adriana enjoyed it when we did things in sync, or at least as close as we could get.

"Leave it to me." Jolene hefted her tool box. "I'm on my way to the police station anyway, or at least the neighborhood." She breezed out of the door.

"Tell me again that you really believe that Grayson is innocent?" Daphne asked.

"Cross my heart and --" I stopped myself before I could finish the sentence. "I do, honestly."

A harassed young mother interrupted us. She held a crying child. "I didn't mean to lose the book," the kid wailed.

We left Daphne to deal with the two.

Chapter Sixteen

The *Carrot Cove* did a brisk business when we reached it.

"I need two green lasagnas," Sally Potts called out over her shoulder.

"Coming right up." Her mother Neely, one of my gelato customers on the day Pierre had acted so strangely, came through a swing door and put two large bowls on the counter. A strand of strawberry blonde hair peeked out from under her hat.

"Where's the dog?" Adriana flitted around the small queue who waited for their turn.

At least half of them used to be Pierre's regulars. They appeared torn between wanting to approach me, probably for gossip, and not wanting to lose their place in the line.

I covered my mouth with my hand. "What dog?" I asked my great-great-aunt.

"They gave away a doggy ball launcher," she reminded me.

That bit of information had almost escaped my mind. There was little likelihood a meat-free business would hand out anything carnivore-related as an advertising gimmick, so there had to be a dog involved.

Which meant another interview partner for Adriana. "I'll come back later," I told the woman closest to me. "I didn't expect such a crowd."

"You and me both." She grimaced. "Their cooking truly has taken off. A few months ago, you'd be able to drop in and be served within five minutes."

"I heard it's that cooking competition," another customer chimed in. "They're all falling over themselves to outdo each other. I'm going to try that *Foodstock* place next." A glance in my direction made them pause awkwardly. "

Not that Pierre wasn't the best. He was," the first woman added.

"No one could beat him in the kitchen, that's for sure," the other customer said. "And I've been told that he was going to maybe partner with one of the others, for the magazine cover, because they like them younger."

I stored away all this information as I sneaked away, to go searching for the animal.

"Wait here," Adriana told me once we'd left the premises and turned into the back alley.

"Why?" Considering that we were surrounded by trash cans, a dumpster, and the backsides of buildings, it was hard to imagine a reason for me to hang around here.

"Because I don't want you to scare her." She gently coaxed a red fox out from behind the bins.

I watched them from a couple of yards away.

The fox growled a little, while her tail worked furiously.

Finally, Adriana called out to me. "We owe her a pound or two of ground beef. The good stuff, not the gristly leftovers the butchers lets you have for your pets."

That stung. "Have you ever seen me get anything but the best for Cleo, or any of your protegées?"

"And we don't want to start now, do we?" She gave me a sweet smile. "This young lady has cubs to feed, too."

"She's got her litter around here?" That spelled trouble. Few people would welcome a family of foxes tearing through their bins and gardens.

"I promised her we'd take her someplace safe," she said. "Once we've fed them."

"And what do we get in return? Or is it just an act of kindness, which is fine, by the way?"

"There was a watchdog, for a couple of days, until the foxy woman sent him away, to our little mama's relief." She nodded towards her new friend who'd made herself invisible except for the tip of her tail. "The woman said, it was unkind to send anyone out in the weather, dog or no dog, and buying dead animals for food was wrong for them."

The foxy woman? "The ginger-haired lady interfered? Neely?"

"As she should. Look around." Adriana sashayed over to a small patch of lawn behind a fence, that belonged to the *Carrot Cove*. A tiny shed offered barely enough shelter for a medium-sized dog. Adriana bopped my nose. "You can use your noodle some more while we do the shopping."

"True." We set off, to reward the fox for her information.

I hoped Adriana had come up with a feasible plan for the relocation and didn't expect me to come up with a solution to keep her promise.

I asked the butcher to wrap the mince in several layers of waxed paper, so I wouldn't end up like a modern version of the pied piper as we headed back to the side alley.

Adriana gave the fox what appeared to be detailed instructions, because the fox started to drag the meat parcel away, without so much as opening it first.

I'd decided to keep out of it. I needed my great-great-aunt to let me in on a conversation soon enough, so it would have been unwise to make her tap into her energy unnecessarily.

"We'll meet them here at midnight," she told me after biding her furry friend farewell. "You'll have to line the trunk with a blanket, and stock up on food."

"Where do we take them?"

"The woods. There's a secluded little grove half a mile from the cove, where Belle and I played hide and seek."

"There used to be one," I corrected her. "It's all part of the golf club now."

"They chopped down my trees? How could they do that?"

"A few are left standing, only the course is open solely for members and their guests. Foxes would definitely not be welcome."

Her face darkened.

"We'll come up with a good place for them," I said.

A taxi went past, distracting me. In the back seat, I'd spotted Grayson. "I think I have an idea who to ask." I kept my fingers crossed that Grayson intended to drop in on Daphne, and I was right.

"She's in the back if you need her." Fred's round face shone with delight at seeing me. "She's got a guest with her, but you won't mind."

I wondered how much Fred knew about our sleuthing. Like with Jolene, little happened in town without him getting an inkling. Thankfully, he tended to be as discreet as he was well-informed.

With Fred manning the front desk, Daphne had closed her office door.

I used the special knock she reserved for close friends. "It's me," I called out, to be on the safe side.

"Come in."

Adriana dashed into the room, with me on her heels.

Grayson gave me a wary shrug. "I swear I did not hurt a hair on my uncle's head. Even the police believed me."

"So they should." Daphne bristled. "To think they'd have the gall to haul you in, despite an alibi. I'm half inclined to call a lawyer friend of mine."

"It's okay," he said. "I'd rather answer a lot of questions than have them put solving the murder on the back burner."

"What alibi?" Adriana asked.

I repeated her question.

"A foaling mare," he said. "I'd planned to have another talk with my uncle, so I drove the thirty miles from my home. Only I hadn't figured out what to say, and instead, I decided to see if Daphne was still awake." He gave her a wistful smile, which she answered with a broad grin.

"But you didn't visit her," I said.

"The lights in her house were out, so I decided to go back home. I was less than five miles out of town when the owner of the horse called."

"Were you on duty?"

"No, but I've been treating this mare since she was foaled, so I was the obvious choice."

"The police said they had a witness who saw Grayson's car on the night in question, and then they found the shoes in the garbage," Daphne said.

"Right monogram, wrong size," he said. "And I'd thought that stenciling your initials into gum boots stopped after school camp."

"The killer tried to play him for a sap," Adriana said.

"Have you made up your mind yet?" Grayson asked me.

"I'll let you know as soon as possible. If your investors are as keen as you say, they won't mind a short delay."

Daphne nodded. "Genie's right. Your clinic is important, but selling your family's legacy to outsiders is a big decision."

I decided to keep silent about having my stepfather put out his feelers, although trying to frame Grayson for the murder was hardly the way to get their hands on *Butler's Pantry*. After all, heirs were prevented from profiting off their crimes, if I remembered my murder mysteries correctly.

"Ask him about the sleeping pills," Adriana said. As a dutiful great-great-niece, I did.

"I had an accident, about a year ago. A cow kicked me and cracked a couple of ribs. Pierre let me stay for a few days, and he got me some pills from his doc. I told the police."

Adriana nudged me.

"One last thing, I have a question about foxes," I said.

He seemed surprised, and so did Daphne.

"Where would you relocate a fox and her young cubs to, so they're safe?" I asked.

"That depends. Are they all well or are they sickly or injured? How old are they?"

Adriana raised her palms. She had no idea.

"They seemed fine, and no idea," I said.

"The problem with urbanized foxes is that it can be tough on them to fend for themselves when our food trash is so much easier to live on."

"We'll ask momma fox," Adriana said.

"I'd be happy to take a look at them," Grayson offered.

Adriana weighed this option.

"Can I get back to you on that one? It might be a bit tricky," I said.

He took my answer in his stride.

"One more thing," I added casually, like an afterthought. "I heard on a couple of occasions that Pierre might have been considering competing at the fair after all, with a partner to act as the official face of the team."

Daphne opened and shut her mouth in surprise.

"Ridiculous." Grayson shook his head. "If there's one thing my uncle was, it was honest. If he'd agreed to give Steve a leg-up - that's who you're talking about, right? - he'd have told me. I had a good talk with the man about Pierre. He looked out for him for me, to see that my uncle didn't overdo it."

That explained the secret meeting behind the dumpster. "I don't think it was Steve," I said.

"In that case, no chance of him doing that. Pierre was as proud as heck of *Butler's Pantry*, and the family recipes. He would never have agreed to use other people's take on food, the same as he would never have allowed anyone outside his closest circle to take credit for his life's work."

"Interesting," I said. "Because that's what I thought too."

"Let's skedaddle," Adriana said. "We've got what we came for."

We took the back exit, with Grayson right behind us.

More and more I approved of him. If he'd stayed until Daphne finished up for the day or waltzed past all the customers, our favorite librarian would find her private life becoming the most researched topic among those of a romantic bent or with a dirty mind. Leaving now meant he was considerate.

"We'll cross him off our list," Adriana said. "That was excellent work, dear gumshoe."

"It was. Now let's see what your usual sources have to say. Maybe we're lucky?"

She wrinkled her nose in surprise.

"Isn't that what Neely said about giving up their dog? That the weather wasn't for anyone to be outside?"

"Except for those who had no choice. Va bene." She preened a little. Our trip to Italy showed once in a while in her vocabulary, when her mood was buoyant. "Let's hop to it."

CHAPTER SEVENTEEN

"I'm not afraid of the big sky bath," Champ boasted. The German Shepherd was the third dog we were interviewing within sight of Pierre's back entrance.

The first two hadn't seen, heard, or smelled anything on the night in question. They'd hunkered down in their dog houses.

Champ was another matter. He shook his whole body to demonstrate how little he cared about being soaked by the rain.

"I bet you're not afraid of anything," Adriana flattered him, her hand on mine so I was part of the conversation.

"Because I'm strong." He flexed his chest muscles, like a canine bodybuilder.

"You were outside all night?" I asked.

He paused, to shift his attention from Adriana to me.

"Leave the talking to me," she whispered. "He likes me better."

So he did, like all the other animals. I wondered if all ghosts (I had to assume there were more around) had that peculiar talent or if my great-great-aunt was special in her pet-whispering abilities.

I hoped for the latter. I liked the idea of others apart from me seeing her as being extraordinary.

"What did you see?" she asked.

Champ covered his eyes with a large paw. "Only the sky bath," he admitted.

My hopes sank.

His paw came down. "And when the water stopped, a human came, covered in a tent."

"Rain gear?" I guessed, in an aside to Adriana.

She repeated my question.

Champ didn't exactly understand the meaning, but he confirmed that a person all hidden underneath garments had entered the building. "It stung my nose when the human came back," he said. "First, he was all delicious, like that." He prodded a half-chewed bone, with strips of meat covering it. "Then he returned, and he stank of fireworks."

"Gunshot residue," Adriana and I said together. "Did you smell anything else, like maybe a cat or a dog?"

That was a good question, one I hadn't thought of.

Champ's ears twitched. "No cat, that much I can say." He chuckled, for lack of a better word. "They're funny, with their little claws and tiny voices."

"They are." Adriana patted him, and he rubbed his head against her hand.

At home, I put on an audiobook for Adriana while I allowed myself a bubble bath.

I trailed my hand through the foam as I thought about what we'd learned. The delicious smell had to be related to cooking, or food prep. I was willing to exclude the *Carrot Cove* gals from my suspect list because Champ would hardly have drooled over vegetables and tofu.

That also meant that we were on the right trail.

Pierre's murder had to be related to the theft of his recipe book.

There were several possible scenarios. One was that the villain thought the book was going to propel them to culinary fame.

Possibility number two was that they wanted to make sure Pierre didn't select a protege, to take part in the competition in his stead.

In scenario number three, they'd simply increased their market share.

I sank deeper into the claw foot tub until the foam covered my ears. "What about Steve?"

I must have spoken out loud. Before I could do so much as work through the train of thoughts that had been bothering me, Adriana popped her head into the bathroom. Only her head, mind. I'd closed the door, and we had an arrangement that she'd ask before entering a room. I needed to make it clear that entering also included using only one body part.

"Did you holler?" she asked.

I reached for the towel. "Give me a minute and I'll be with you."

"Do you want coffee? I could do with one." Her head disappeared.

I hastened to towel off and wrapped myself in my dressing gown.

I found her staring lovingly at the percolating coffee maker.

Cleo rested in her kitchenette cat basket. So far, only the bathroom had no designated sleeping spot for her. For now.

I repeated my question as I filled my mug. "What about Steve?"

She sniffed at the brew. "No milk?"

I added a splash.

Cleo raised her head, only to decide she wasn't that interested in moving herself.

"What about him?" she asked.

"How do you think he honestly felt about Pierre? He did most of the work as a chef, and yet whenever the boss came to add his secret ingredients, he had to leave the kitchen. That must have stung."

A tiny crease showed on her forehead as she pondered the question. "There was an issue, with him and Tammy. At least, I think there was. Remember our girls' night out?"

"You swung from the chandelier. That'd be hard to forget."

"That bit was the bee's knees." She giggled.

I waited.

Adriana had a memory that'd be the envy of an elephant. Only today, it let her down.

I cursed myself that I'd ignored it when she mentioned that something'd been up with Steve.

She massaged her temples. "It's all fuzzy. There was the crowd and the music and my tastebuds tingled."

"That was the booze."

"Right." She clapped her hands. "That's what's missing. If we could set the scene then I'm sure it'll come back to me in a flash."

"I could mix us an Aperol spritz," I suggested. Since Italy, we'd both become fond of the cocktail.

For Adriana, it was the prosecco that went into it.

For me, it was the chance, to only add a splash of alcohol to a drink famous for its versatility. Since my great-great-aunt tended to be tipsy after a few deep breaths of wine, anything more than a thimbleful was overkill. I'd become used to minimal alcohol without losing any of the fun.

She stopped me as I took out the Aperol bottle. "I need the whole shebang. The dames, the tunes, the razzle-dazzle." She swayed to music only she could hear.

"Give me a chance." I mixed a weak version of the cocktail and held it under her nose.

Adriana's nose twitched. A dreamy smile spread over her face.

"And?" I asked, full of hope.

"Nothing."

"Try again."

She stuck her nose in the glass and giggled.

"Do you remember now?"

"Only that I really like this."

Frustrated, I pulled away the glass and emptied it into the sink.

"I'm sorry," she said.

"It's okay. I'll take care of it." My phone pinged the same instant my mom knocked on my door.

Aimée said, "We're back, and Tony has news for you."

I changed into jeans and a white shirt. Then, Adriana and I raced downstairs.

After the first few steps, she hopped onto the banister and slid down. "Wooohoo. You've got to try this."

I decided to decline that tempting suggestion, at least in public, which since the arrival of my merry ancestress, included my mother.

Tony had switched into business mode, complete with wire-rimmed spectacles and a folder with spreadsheets.

Some of the papers I recognized from the material Grayson had sent me. I took the seat next to him at the butcher block table that served as a mobile workstation and prepping area.

"The good news is, the offer is legitimate," he said. "They're interested in expanding into casual dining, and *Butler's Pantry* is an obvious choice. It used to have ex-cellent turnover when Pierre opened it as a real restau-rant on weekend evenings, and it's got almost classic status, without any of the big chain trappings. They'd only need minimal investment in the whole set-up."

"That makes sense. What's the bad news?"

"They can't pinpoint exactly who came up with the idea of approaching the nephew. It's one of these occasions where suddenly an idea is in the air."

"I see."

"Applesauce," Adriana muttered.

"Did you hear anything about how they stumbled upon Pierre's?"

"He's been a well-known figure in the gastro scene forever, so that's one explanation. All I can tell you is that this company started looking into it when the whole idea of the fair came up, with this influx of new small businesses while you were in Italy. I guess they thought Cobblewood Cove is going to end up on a lot of people's radar, plus there is an opening here for their kind of enterprise."

"Do you believe that?"

Tony showed me the figures for the forecast profits on the spreadsheets.

I gaped. I'd be happy to make in a year what they thought they could bring in, in a month.

"It might put a few other people out of business, if this goes ahead," Tony said.

"Like newcomers already struggling with making their mark?"

"With Pierre around, it was always going to be doable but tough," my mother said. "You' 'd have to be more than optimistic or bring in a whole new sort of customer to compete, which in a small town is close to requiring a miracle." She reached for Tony's hand. "Even I have a hard time imagining this place without Pierre, and I adore a certain change of scenery."

Adriana guffawed again, either because the Prosecco hadn't quite worn off, or because my mother's words came close to the understatement of the year.

When I was growing up, we had two taped-up boxes we carried with us from move to move. They never got opened, as an unconscious sign that we hadn't settled for good yet. I still didn't know what Aimée had kept in those boxes, or if they stood in some storage space as I remembered them, untouched for decades.

"Are you fine with us leaving for a day or two? We've been invited to a gallery opening", Aimée said. "Or is there anything else we can do?" Her face shone with eagerness, and so did Tony's.

I could have told them sleuthing only felt like fun when you were as far removed as possible from a killer intent on silencing you. I had more than enough experience with that.

Even Adriana, who no longer had to fear for her life, looked aghast. "Tell them to leave it to us," she said. "Two Darling detectives are enough."

"If anything comes up, I'll get in touch," I said. "It's mostly background things I'm checking on, in case the police miss stuff."

My mom bestowed two air kisses on me and mimed me phoning her.

I waved them goodbye and added a few questions to my growing list.

Adriana read them while I prepared for girls' night out, the sequel. "I wish Matt was here," she said. "He's a swell dancer."

I didn't know what to reply, so I said nothing.

Chapter Eighteen

I still hadn't made up my mind if I missed Matt more or if the relief of not having to explain Adriana's existence yet outweighed his absence, when Jolene brought the subject up as well.

I'd barely reached our table at the *Vine and Vinyl*, when she asked me, "Is there a problem with you and my cousin?"

Adriana gasped. "No! He's not dumping you?"

We all shivered as my great-great-aunt unleashed a chill, a clear sign she was shaken by the idea.

If I was honest, so was I. "Why are you asking? Did he mention anything?" I sank onto a chair.

Jolene signaled to Olivia and her business partner who sat chatting at the *Foodstock* counter, that we were good for now. "It's just that it feels weird to have him go on so many trips, and you don't seem bothered."

"Honestly, with all that's going on, it's hard to find space to breathe, let alone worry about Matt," I admitted.

"Who said worry?" Daphne breezed in, still dressed in her comfortable combination of slacks and sweater. She fit right in with most of the customers.

Although the same music as on pizza night played in the background, and an array of vintage photographs gave the place a certain vibe the Goodge's had borrowed from *Butler's Pantry*, the buzz of a party with live music was missing.

That wasn't good at all if Adriana needed to recreate the evening as closely as possible.

The *Foodstock* part had less than a dozen customers, and a teenage waiter served them. Olivia and Katie must be on their break from the kitchen before it got busy again if it did get busy.

Felix rearranged the vinyl records.

Adriana split her attention between him and Jolene. It was hard to tell if she searched for hints of guilt on his part, or the signs of a growing affection. As much as my great-great-aunt loved to play the hardnosed sleuth, her romantic tendencies were at least as strongly developed.

Daphne had a tiny swagger in her step, so she had recovered from her earlier upset.

"I'll head to the bar. What did you have last time?" I asked.

"It's a bit early for strong drinks. Coffee would be great. Or a beer."

Adriana gulped at the mention of her least favorite alcoholic beverage.

"How about a bottle of wine? I'll buy," I suggested.

"Fine with me," Jolene said.

Daphne gave in.

I ordered a bottle of Californian Merlot from the waitress and asked her to bring three glasses.

"The kitchen will open again in half an hour," Katie told me. She joined the waitress.

"We're good, thanks." I handed over my credit card when the sweet odor of roses hit my nose.

The Schuyler sisters had arrived.

"How lovely to see you," I said.

"We're so happy we simply had to come and visit with you girls," Primrose said.

Her sister tittered. "It's such wonderful news that Pierre's nephew has been cleared. I assume you're celebrating?" Her gaze wandered towards our table, and Daphne.

I got the impression the Schuylers had also picked up on the budding relationship.

A corkscrew clanked as it hit the floor. Katie apologized for startling us.

"What shall we two have?" Primrose asked her sister.

"Make it five glasses," I told the waitress.

Daphne and Jolene had already added two chairs to our table.

Adriana circled us like a hungry shark, taking a whiff here and there. Her movements slowed down a little.

"Close your eyes," I whispered, with my hand covering my mouth. "Try to see everything as it was, with Steve and Tammy."

"What are you saying?" Jolene frowned at me.

"I was talking to myself. Mental notes."

"Smart," Adriana said. She covered her face with both hands and did a pirouette. "Got it." She inhaled the boozy aroma once more, and off she was, shimmying around the room, past the record cabinet, the jukebox, the photos, and the table where Steve and his fiancé had spent the evening. She opened her eyes and stared at the photos, obviously taking in every inch of the place.

"Is it really official that Grayson's no longer a suspect?" Daphne asked.

"We have it from the highest authority," Primrose told her. "His alibi has been confirmed by the mayor's niece. He was at her farm at the crucial hour."

"I love to think that Pierre will be at peace now, with his own flesh and blood innocent. And we do hope that young Grayson can open his free clinic. Such a wonderful idea," her sister said.

"You knew?" I could have saved myself the question. Of course, they did.

"The young man spoke to Petey's veterinarian first, and Pierre came to us, to talk things over," Primrose said. "He wasn't as fit as he used to be, and he loved animals."

That much was true. He'd kept a few containers for meat scraps and marrow bones, which he handed over to dog and cat owners. Still, I hadn't received the impression that he cared much for Grayson's causes when they fought about the future of *Butler's Pantry*.

Adriana was singing now. She made up the lyrics herself, although she stuck to the tune of *Girl from Ipanema*, which played in the background. "Swell and cute the Darling detectives will come for thugs without an invective", she crooned.

I hoped she or I'd remember those lyrics when we came home. She'd never forgive me if they didn't end up in her collected literary works.

"What do you think is the best way forward?" I asked the sisters. They'd been among Pierre's oldest friends, and if anyone had an idea what decision he'd have wanted me to make, they were top of the list.

"That's a difficult question. He struggled a little with all the changes,," Primrose said.

Her sister chimed in, "He used to say, maybe the era of good, honest food is over. With prices going up so much, he said he felt bad about charging more, yet he also felt bad at having to consider twice if the business allowed him to raise wages. He counted himself lucky that Steve stuck it out."

The two sisters, who'd never lacked money, sighed.

"Maybe that's why he didn't pick a successor," Jolene said. "He thought he was the last of his kind."

"If he worried about money, why did he rent me that space for next to nothing?" I asked.

"To help you on your feet." Primrose sipped her wine. "He said you were like a granddaughter to him."

"Maybe that's what he wanted as his legacy," Daphne said. "To have you find your way, without the burden of the past."

We commiserated in silence. Had Pierre, who'd been so proud of the family history, really wanted it to end with him?

I noticed Adriana aiming for the chandelier. "I think we should call it a day," I said loud enough for her to register. "The dinner crowd's on its way."

Right in cue, two large groups came in.

Felix rushed over to the *Foodstock* side, to push together tables. He glanced back over his shoulder.

Jolene waved at him but joined the rest of us as we grabbed our coats.

Outside, stars twinkled in the inky sky. A golden haze swirled around the street lamps.

Adriana sang under her breath. "Swell and cute ..." She floated a few inches above the ground.

I hoped the wine had triggered her memory enough to tell me what had been going on with Steve and his fiancée.

Daphne wrapped herself tighter into her jacket. "Did Hank talk to you about developments in the case, apart from the good news about Grayson?"

We broke into a brisk walk, to ward off the cold. Adriana snuggled up to me.

"Only that they're pursuing every lead, whatever that means," Jolene said.

The Schuylers each clasped one of my hands. "We'll see you soon. We don't want to sound callous, but have you thought about our bespoke ice cream flavor? We promised to host a special celebration after the trophies are handed over," Primrose said.

"I'm on it," I said. "Give me a few more days."

"Lovely." They both gently patted my cheek, to say goodnight.

"It's hard to imagine the fair without Pierre," Jolene said.

"Why? He wasn't going to take part, apart from the stall, and I don't think he'd run that himself," I pointed out.

"He did a lot of the work in the background." Daphne sped up her walking. "Without the fair, we'd have a lot fewer new businesses."

I thought back to Tony's spreadsheets. "There are definitely people who stood to gain a lot by seeing Pierre out of the way."

"It's not as if they'd be likely to have known that when they moved to Cobblewood Cove," she pointed out.

"Unless they did. I mean, if you start somewhere, wouldn't you try to settle for a place without overwhelming competition? Unless you have deep pockets and no burning need to end up in the black at the end of every week."

Adriana hiccuped. "Stop spinning, Genie." Her head lolled on my shoulder. My great-great-aunt was drunk.

How could she have gotten worse, after we'd left *Vine and Vinyl*? My gaze fell onto the ground. An unscrewed plastic bottle with rubbing alcohol lay next to my feet, outside the pharmacy. I picked it up with a tissue and searched around for the cap, to stop Adriana from inhaling more of the fumes.

"Here." Jolene bent and held up the cap. "Do you think we should sprinkle sand where this was, to soak up any spillage, before an animal licks it up?"

Adriana's chin sank onto her chest. Her legs buckled until I caught her. Uh-oh.

"Can I leave you to it?" I asked. "I've got an important thing to take care of."

"That was a short girls' night out," Jolene said.

"Come back to my place," I suggested. "I'll only need a few minutes first." If my friends thought I was acting weird, I couldn't help it. I had no idea what Adriana's soused state could do to her if I didn't ground her fast. If we were lucky, her clothes and the brick in my purse were enough. I'd rather not push it though.

I wished I'd taken my car. When we'd set out, I thought it better to walk, in case I had a second glass of wine. Now I regretted my caution.

"Slow down, I'm woozy," Adriana said.

A dog barked at me.

"See, he says so too," she said.

"I have to take her home," I told the dog. He stopped barking.

I should have been able to understand him, while I was holding my great-great-aunt, I thought bewildered. It was a bad sign that that connection had broken down.

CHAPTER NINETEEN

For an as good as weightless ghost she was hard to manoeuver up the stairs.

Cleo growled at me.

"It wasn't my fault," I said.

She growled again.

"I'll be swell if I have a rest," Adriana said.

Together, we stumbled to the sofa, with Cleo weaving figures of eight between our legs.

"Did you remember everything?"

She nodded, only to wince. "What was that stuff? It's worse than moonshine."

"It wasn't meant for drinking. Or inhaling."

The doorbell rang. I buzzed our friends in.

"Quick, tell me before you forget," I said to my great-great-aunt.

"Can a girl sort through her thoughts first?" Her pale hand fluttered to her forehead in a performance worthy of a golden-age movie heroine.

"As long as you keep focussed. Tell Cleo, to be on the safe side."

I kept my fingers crossed that ghost and cat together would deliver the information and that Adriana's memory wasn't linked too closely to places or levels of intoxication.

Jolene came in alone. "Daphne decided she had to go home and spend the evening with her dog."

Cleo meowed.

"I think your cat approves," Jolene said.

Cleo stretched.

"She's the smartest cat I've met." I stroked the soft head.

The little tabby loved compliments just as much as her favorite Darling, who'd rolled onto her back and appeared to be conducting an invisible orchestra with her hands.

"I won't stay too long either," Jolene said.

"Do you want a drink?" She only had to answer a few questions, and then I'd be happy to return to my ghost-sitting duties.

"Tea would be fine." She opened the cupboard and took out two of Jilly's hand-crafted mugs. One carried the inscription, 'Teatillating', the other read 'Teatotal'. Jilly had created them while in her whimsical phase.

Jolene peered out of the window. "Does it ever feel to you like none of this is really happening?"

Adriana's hand stopped conducting. "What's up with her?"

That was a good question. Jolene was the most un-flappable, resolutely down-to-earth person in my life. She dealt in pragmatical things, and to hear her delving into philosophy gave me a strange sensation.

I set her mug down on the windowsill.

Jolene warmed her hands on it. "Less than a week ago, everything was so clean cut. We knew who people were and what to expect from them."

"She's talking about the pianist." Adriana sat upright and swung around to face us. The rubbing alcohol had worn off.

"People are always good for surprises," I said. "We all have secrets, even if they're perfectly harmless."

"Ain't that the truth," Jolene said.

Cleo curled up next to my great-great-aunt, with an air of smugness. I could be wrong, but I reckoned she en-joyed her special status as keeper of human and ghostly secrets, and four-legged confidante.

"We probably all hope that Pierre will have been killed by a person we don't care about. It'd be nice to see Cobblewood Cove in the headlines and on the magazine cover because of the fair and the cooking competition, not because of a homicide." Jolene heaved a deep sigh.

I sipped my tea.

"I heard Miss Lulu has kept a whole day free in her schedule, to style the winner. That's her contribution to the big event," Jolene said.

"In that case, we'd better hope that it's a woman who'll triumph. If she's got to deal with Steve or worse, a bald guy, she'll cry over her hot rollers. Olivia'd look good."

"Not a chance. She's out." "

She is?" Adriana and I shared a meaningful glance.

"She doesn't like her picture taken, Felix told me. She's going to leave that sort of publicity to the other gal."

"Doesn't that strike you as odd?"

Jolene squirmed. "There's a reason."

"Spill it, sister." Adriana sashayed over to us.

Cleo traipsed after her.

"A reason," I repeated.

"You've got to promise me you won't tell anyone."

"I promise. Unless --"

"It's got nothing to do with Pierre." She glowered at me, another first.

"Then you have my word."

"Goodge is not her real name. Their parents married after she was born, and she kept her mom's maiden name. Only Felix is a real Goodge."

I still was no wiser as to why that was such a big deal.

"They came here to hide from her ex. A new start, far away, among new people."

"And a nationwide magazine cover with her picture on it would blow that." Now I understood.

"That's why they're so evasive about where they're from. They're not even on social media."

"Yet he confided in you."

Adriana hovered over the windowsill. "Now we're getting to the good stuff. She's blushing."

"No prying," I mouthed.

Jolene gave me a blank stare.

I beamed at her. People loved to fill in the bits for you if you gave them half a chance, I'd discovered.

"It was less confiding and more explaining about the name on the money transfer to pay for materials."

Yes, her cheeks had a pinker tinge than usual. I wished I could cross the Goodges off my list, for Jolene's sake. Alas, that would have been premature. They still stood to gain a lot with Pierre out of the picture. That brought me to my last question. "Why did they settle on Cobblewood Cove?"

"I told you I was sort of recommending it," she said.

"Which is fine for a place like Felix's. But for his sister to compete with *Butler's Pantry* was ambitious unless they have a well-padded bank account. That is if they had any clue about the competition."

"I gave him all the facts, and the rest is up to them and their accountant. Anyway, they've both got an alibi. Sort of."

"They do? That's great."

"Except, they're it. For each other. When the rain set in, Felix decided to bunk on his sister's couch."

"Some alibi," Adriana muttered.

I agreed. Unless one of my great-great-aunt's four-legged sources confirmed their whereabouts, the Goodges stayed on my suspect list. Still, I decided to cheer Jolene up as she took her leave. "With or without Felix, I think doing up the old speakeasy is a great idea."

"I hope so. Otherwise, it feels like a recipe for disaster, sinking all my savings into a project when I'm missing the secret sauce." She stared into the dregs of her tea.

Her words stirred up a vague idea in my mind. Sadly, it resisted becoming fully formed at this moment.

"That girl is going to be in trouble if she can't decide if she wants that swell pianist to serenade her or the whole town," Adriana said once Jolene was out of the door.

"The sooner we have this mess sorted out, the better."

"It's absurd. The only person we had on our radar who wasn't dear to any of our friends is out of the question."

"Who?"

"The *Carrot Cove* people? Your buddy Champ's nose has cleared them. They'd hardly smell of meat."

"Maybe yes and maybe no." She allowed herself a dramatic pause.

I resigned myself to waiting until she was satisfied with herself. I made a list of our stock of gelato ingredients while my great-great-aunt enjoyed her long special moment.

She cleared her throat.

I put my notes aside.

"You forgot one person."

"Like, who?"

"Tammy."

"Steve's fiancée?" I rubbed my hands in glee. Good grief, I was fast becoming a walking cliché. Then again, Tammy had been doubting my innocence.

"Give me two chairs," Adriana said.

I did as I was told. The lights flickered. It took me a heartbeat to figure out that my great-great-aunt played around with the power until she was happy with the wattage. Adriana was setting her scene.

She leaned forward in her chair, changing her voice to a spot-on impression of Tammy's. "You've got to make him see your way."

In a blink, she'd switched seats. Now she sounded more like Steve. "I'm fine the way things are."

Another change of chairs, and she was Tammy again. "And you expect me to be happy with you playing second fiddle to an old dude in a second-rate town? You should be his partner, and if he's too decrepit or too much of a coward to take the heat in this competition, well, then it's overdue that he gets out of the kitchen."

Adriana paused. Channeling herself she said, "That's when she waved around that magazine."

"What did Steve say?"

She switched seats and lowered her pitch. "Honey, we've been through this. I've got enough on my plate with my restoration and mastering brewing skills. It's no big deal if I don't have a trophy."

Again, she switched into Tammy's role. "No big deal? This means big money, and if you learn Pierre's secrets --"

"That's not going to happen." Adriana, aka Steve, took on a defiant tone.

She became Tammy. "Well, it'd better. Or you'll find yourself sharing your bedroom with only that mutt you took in when I'm gone."

Another switch of persona. "Is it your new best friend over there who's been giving you ideas?"

Adriana hopped off the chair. "That's when things became a bit of a blur for me."

"Tammy," I pondered.

"It could have been her," Adriana declared. "Dollars to donuts Steve had told her a lot about Pierre's habits, like keeping his secrets all locked up. And when she couldn't steal the book --" Adriana mimed firing a gun.

"That first break-in that didn't make much sense? You think that was her?" It fit. If Tammy'd been disturbed in Pierre's office, all she had to say was that she was waiting for her fiancé, or cut herself and was searching for a bandage.

"She really was peeved about the dog, and she ranted about him still vaping, after she told hom to stop," Adriana said. "Who could dislike a dog? Good on Steve for taking him off the Pottses hands, and good riddance to her." She glanced at my notes. "Do we need to churn another batch tonight?"

"Unless I set my alarm for the crack of dawn."

She wiggled her fingers. "I feel like creating a new ice cream sort. We'll call it, *PawPaws' Pleasure*." She waited for my reaction.

"You're the boss," I said. "What do I need to put on the table?"

She gave me a sad little head-shake. "*PawPaws' Pleasure*. Like, paws? Cats? Dogs?"

"That's such a clever name," I enthused, hoping that would satisfy her. "I was a little distracted, by an idea I had."

"For ice cream?" Now I allowed myself a little smugness.

"A bit more than that. I'll let it stew and then I'll tell you."

CHAPTER TWENTY

The first birds sang in the trees as I dragged myself out of the house.

Adriana was in a cheerful mood, in stark contrast to sleep-deprived me.

The cold interior of the car, in combination with the cold gelato containers, made things worse for me.

Adriana gave me a reproachful once over. "Not exactly sunny Jim, are you? Or sunny Jane." She chortled at her wit.

Ambulance sirens interrupted her. "Follow that car!" she called out.

"And then what?"

"Don't pretend to be a dumb Dora. Don't you want to see what's going on?"

"Only if you stop that silly name-calling." To please my great-great-aunt, I turned in the direction the ambulance had gone. It took us to the end of Main Street.

The sirens stopped. So had our target. The paramedics had parked outside the *Carrot Cove* and were now hurrying around the back

"Ominous," Adriana said.

My mouth went dry. "Very."

"I see someone. Wait here."

"Let me park first," I said.

Too late. She'd oozed through the door, to communicate with a cat perched on a fence.

I felt the onset of a headache as I squeezed my Toyota into a free space at the curb and left the vehicle in the traditional manner.

"What took you so long?" Adriana said as I caught up. The cat curled her tail around her body and Adriana's arm.

"The laws of the human world?"

"We can't dilly-dally when a murderer's on the loose."

A chill crept up my spine, intensified by the fact that I'd already been cold. "What do you mean? Is there another dead body?"

"We can't be sure yet, but Neely has been screaming bloody murder when my friend here came out for her morning hunt."

I still pondered this when the paramedics returned, with a covered form on the stretcher between them. They loaded their freight into the back of the ambulance and switched on the sirens again.

"That's a good sign," I said. "They wouldn't do that for a corpse."

A police car came screeching along.

I decided to get out of the way. We'd hear soon enough what on earth was going on. Had I been wrong?

Outside Pierre's backdoor, I couldn't bring myself to open it yet. I'd have given a lot to be able to unlock it, saunter in, and see my old friend in his old apron and wielding a chopping knife.

"We've got this," Adriana said. "We're the derring-do Darlings."

I turned the key, took a deep, grounding breath, and exhaled slowly, my eyes firmly shut. I opened them only after I'd crossed the threshold - and stared straight into Steve's face.

We both took a step back.

"I didn't mean to startle you," he said. His hands twisted his chef's hat.

"What are you doing here?"

"I came here to pick up a few things. Grayson said it was okay." His skin had a greyish tint, and his clothes held a faint odor of beer.

"Any plans what you're going to do now?" I asked. "Open your brewery?"

"I haven't decided. I'm so used to having Pierre as a sounding board."

"And without him, you're lost. Me too." I felt a little ashamed to use his obvious pain to fish for information.

Adriana had less restraint. "Ask him about Tammy."

I did. "What about your fiancée? I heard that she was excited for you to take on a bigger role? Do you want to take over here?"

His eye twitched. "We haven't been on the same page lately if you must know. That's part of why I'm here, to see if I can sit in the kitchen and clear my head. What about you? Grayson said you haven't made up your mind what's going to happen next with this place."

I followed him into the kitchen, where everything looked like I remembered it, with the glaring exception of the owner. "What would you think best?"

"I'd hate to see *Butler's Pantry* closing. I'd also hate to see it being run by a stranger."

"And Tammy?" I asked.

His face darkened. "It's like she's got this big idea about me becoming an important chef, like the one she sees on television, where everyone is in awe of them and they drive a fancy car and live in a mansion. She didn't use to be like that before these new people came to town."

"Could you take over, if a new owner would ask you?"

"I told Grayson I can do the cooking alright, blindfold-ed. What I can't do is add the little twists that made Pierre and his pa and grandpa before him legends. That's a fact, Genie. Only Tammy doesn't understand that. I --" His phone rang. "Yes?"

I stepped away, to give him privacy.

Adriana decided to press her ear against his phone to eavesdrop.

Steve's breath became ragged. "I don't believe it." He ended the call, shaking. His gaze found me in the doorway to the main room. "Tammy says they've got the killer. The woman tried to commit suicide."

"She?"

"The younger of the *Carrot Cove* duo. And for what, a lousy moment in the spotlight?" He slammed his hand on the marble worktop and winced. "It's incredible."

"Baloney, that's what it is," Adriana declared.

"I've got to go," Steve said. "Tammy was real upset."

"And I'm the queen of England," my great-great-aunt muttered.

"Isn't she glad it's over?" I asked Steve.

"She will be, once it's sunk in, and the magazine people say the contest will still go ahead." He had the decency to flinch. "She didn't mean it like that, I'm sure."

"We're all a bit on edge." A vague smile accompanied my words.

"You can say that again. Oh, and one other thing. I should have done it sooner, I know, but I clean forgot."

"Yes?"

"There's a copy of the recipes Pierre had me learn in the pantry, in one of the flour containers. The secret parts are missing, but the rest's all written down." He noticed my confusion. "It's an empty container, and the book has been there for years unless Pierre removed it."

With that, he left, and Adriana and I could do what we'd come for.

"We are still using this trap?" Adriana asked. "Or do you believe that the police have the killer?"

"Not likely." A message hit my inbox. I read it. "Jolene says she heard it was an overdose of sleeping pills, the same sort that was mixed into Pierre's brandy." I shivered. "The murderer must have decided to switch scapegoats after Grayson had a solid alibi."

Adriana left the pantry, and the search for the recipes, to me, while she did a little reconnoiter of her own. She called out to me as I lifted an oilcloth-wrapped book out of a tin. "You've got to clap your peepers on this."

I found her standing in front of the old photos, tapping on the group picture with all the staff from right before World War 2.

Pierre's dad and granddad were flanked by a wiry guy with a shock of dark hair and a tall flaxen-haired man.

Adriana's mouth set in a grim line. "Do you recognize that fella?"

"Not that I can say. Which one do you mean?"

"The blond one. There's a picture of him hanging on the wall of *Vine and Vinyl*, with another bunch of men."

At the bottom of the picture, a row of names was written in faded ink. I squinted to decipher it.

"Lars Johansson. There were a lot of Scandinavians around," she said.

"Who went on to have families and friends, I assume."

"This would explain the interest in Cobblewood Cove, but not why they all were so focused on hiding a connection. Having roots here counts for a lot. I'm proof of that."

"Except if it would also incriminate you." I took the framed picture down and stowed it away in my tote, for safekeeping.

If we were right, we had no time to lose. Should the latest victim pull through, I was convinced the killer would strike again, until they felt safe.

My heart pounded against my ribs as I thought of the stretcher and the still body lying on it. If the worst happened and the young woman died, the police would be happy to close the case.

I couldn't allow that to happen. Dead or not, she deserved the truth. Pierre deserved it.

Aimée confirmed her and Tony's support while they were still in the big smoke, for the gallery opening.

My instructions had been clear and simple. Now I prayed that the bait in my trap would be enough to catch a murderer.

Chapter Twenty-One

Adriana sneezed, a fake sneeze that made Cleo recoil and me laugh until I covered myself in a light dusting of turmeric powder.

Now I sneezed, and Cleo fled onto the top of the kitchen cupboard.

"Take a pinch," my great-great-aunt ordered. She inspected the tiny amount of turmeric powder I'd scooped onto the smallest measuring spoon we used for our gelato. Her nostrils twitched. She moved over to the pot with beef stew simmering on the stove. "Half the amount."

With utmost precision, I divided the amount of spice.

"Stir it in," she said.

The turmeric was the last ingredient I'd added to the pot. On the kitchen counter stood a dozen spices, all items Pierre had purchased regularly.

"Are we done?" I wiped my hands on a piece of kitchen towel.

"Patience," said the ghost who so far hadn't shown the smallest inkling of possessing that virtue. "The sniff test takes a little while."

"It's almost midnight." We'd already spent hours in my kitchen, doing our best to reverse-engineer at least one of Pierre's older recipes. "It doesn't have to be perfect, only close enough to pass as one of his."

She fake-sneezed again. "That's better. I still had cloves clogging up my beak."

Since all I'd done was follow her every instruction, I had no intention of taking responsibility for anything happening to her spectral nose. Among other considerations, we'd agreed that her superior abilities were the only chance we had to recreate a recipe worth killing for.

Our choice had been limited to the dishes I'd brought home from *Butler's Pantry*, and to ones I'd be able to cook using the book from the flour tin. This was our second dish. The better of the two would win out.

"Give me a sample," Adriana said. I dipped a ladle into the pot and held it under her nose. Her nostrils flared.

Cleo drooled.

"This is too spicy for you," I told the cat.

"Genie's right," Adriana confirmed. "You'll have the meat without the sauce. Otherwise, we're done here."

Cleo jumped off the cupboard and flopped onto the ground, next to her bowl. She licked her lips.

"One piece," I said. "And then we'll have to go." I cut a chunk of beef into tiny cubes. "Repeat the spices once more," I said to Adriana.

She listed them in an orderly fashion, and I wrote them down, copying Pierre's neat handwriting.

Then I took a container of mince out of the fridge. Adriana and I had a promise to keep.

The fox family came out of hiding after Adriana's second call. The mother carried her cubs one by one into the trunk, which I'd bolstered with blankets.

My palms became sweaty as we drove through the night, to the nearest wildlife sanctuary. Grayson had reassured us that the little family would be safe there.

It was the best we could do. Afterwards, we only had one small job left to take care of.

Tony polished the windscreen of his Audi when Adriana and I came down, after a too short rest. He and Aimée must have been setting off before daybreak.

I was touched.

"I've dropped your mom off at the hairdresser's, as requested," he said.

"That's great."

"Is there anything else we can do? There are a few more favors I can call in." He inspected his handiwork. "Do you see streaks?"

I pointed out one, and he reached for the windscreen cleaner. Aimée had warned me that Tony cleaned his car whenever he was nervous.

"Tony?"

He paused, with the bottle in his hand.

"No need to worry. It'll be fine, and Mom will have a ball."

I said the same words to Daphne. She'd agreed to meet me at *Vine & Vinyl* where I asked Felix to help me find a few recordings of 1920s and 1930s tunes, while I studied the photos on the wall.

Adriana had been right, flaxen-haired Johansson appeared in two of them. In one he was stirring a gallon-sized pot, in the other, he wore a uniform.

Felix jumped to it with the eagerness of a true enthusiast, and Daphne and I wandered through to *Foodstock*, where I ordered a takeaway pizza.

"I only hope my mother won't go completely overboard," I said. "The spotlight should still be on the fair and the competition." I lowered my voice to a conspiratorial level while keeping it loud enough to be overheard if any of the staff was so inclined. "I think she hopes that her guest of honor, Tony's TV producer friend, gives the open spot on his new cooking slot to the local talent."

"If there's any chefs left standing. I can't get my head around Sallie Potts killing Pierre in cold blood. She must have known the gig is up when she took the sleeping pills. She's in a coma, Fred told me."

"How does he know?"

"One of the nurses came into the library to borrow a few romance novels." Daphne lifted her hand and asked for an alcohol-free beer while we waited. "Aimée might be disappointed. There's not much local kitchen talent around."

"She's pinning her hopes on whoever bags the catering job for her soirée. Which reminds me." I waved at Olivia, who stood discussing something with Katie.

Adriana kept watch over them.

"Would it be okay if I leave you a few flyers here? Or do you know of a top-notch chef who'd be up for a last-minute catering job, for a VIP party? It's the night before the big cooking contest, so you'll probably be too busy," I said.

"That depends." Olivia all but ripped my carefully crafted flyer out of my hand.

"The payment will be more than adequate. Tony's never stingy."

"It's very last minute," Daphne said. "I thought your mom would have spent the last month, pulling out all the stops for her party planning."

I lowered my gaze to the ground, the picture of soulfulness. "She wanted Pierre to shine, that's why she invited tv network people who could make him a star on national level. It took a lot of convincing from Tony to arrange this party at all. It was only when I found the two recipes left for me, that she came around."

"You found what?"

"When I'm saying recipes, it's more like a postscript, listing all the ingredients and steps Pierre took care of, once Steve had done all the prep work. But, yeah, if Steve gives me the recipe from the original cookbook, it should work. Except that, I told Aimée that gelato-making is good enough for me. I have no intention to become a celebrity chef or to be on television pretending to be one. That's why I left Pierre's gift to me where I found it, taped to the inside of my order book behind his counter."

Daphne took a flyer too. "That's such a sweet gift. Would you like me to put this up in the library?"

"If that's okay? My mom is going to hold the audition for the job tomorrow night. Otherwise, she'll go with Tony's regular caterer."

"Pizza's ready." Katie handed me the box, and I left with Daphne.

Adriana stayed behind. If Olivia and Katie had something to discuss, she planned to witness it.

I stopped outside, waiting for my great-great-aunt.

"Aren't you coming?" Daphne asked. "The pizza's not getting any warmer."

I chuckled. "If you hold it for me, I'll quickly check that I haven't forgotten a task. I hate it when I remember the moment I arrive back home."

"I'm the same." Daphne took the carton from me while I pretended to scroll through my phone.

Adriana shimmied through the closed door. "They're both gung-ho about the job, but nothing suspicious. We can skedaddle."

Aimée returned to the Darling villa a little later than we did, brimming with enthusiasm and showing me her newly manicured nails. "Miss Lulu's done a great job. I might make this a regular thing."

"That's nice," I said. "You did spread the news?"

"Of course I did. And in a very natural way, too, if I may say so."

Adriana peered at my mother's fingernails, slid off her metaphysical opera glove, and compared them to her own almond-shaped nails. "Not bad," she said. "If your mother stuck to the script."

"I assume Miss Lulu swallowed the bait?" I asked Aimée.

"Trust me, by the end of the night there won't be a single soul left who hasn't heard about my little soirée and your discovery." A worried frown flickered over my mother's face. "You're not going to take any risks?"

"I'll be safe." I covered her hand with mine. "We'll all be safe."

All, except for Sallie Potts, who was still in hospital, fighting for her life.

If only I'd been faster at connecting the dots, she'd never have been in danger. I squeezed Aimée's hand. "I'll see you tomorrow."

Adriana wooshed up the railing, a new trick that I failed to admire.

I had too much on my mind for that. Had we covered all the angles or had I overlooked any details?

Chapter Twenty-Two

Four prospective caterers had signed up for a shot at Aimée's gig.

We'd given out 15-minute slots. Apart from my mother, the tasting judges consisted of the Schuyler sisters and Steve.

I'd roped him in when he failed to apply for the job.

He perched on a stool in a corner. Small plates and bowls and a large box full of cutlery sat on a large table in the large tent that had been erected only this morning, for the fair. By the side stood a table full of kitchen tools.

My tongue stuck to the roof of my mouth.

I took a swig of water. It didn't help.

"It's all going to be dandy." Adriana fluttered around, checking every inch of the grand tent which had been modeled after the one in the baking shows on TV.

Five oversized stoves sat side by side, with worktops between them.

They'd come into their own for the competition. Today, the caterers were allowed to bring their already-prepared dishes.

I paced around.

"Stop it. People will see you and notice that something's up."

I forced myself to relax.

"Are we ready?" Dahlia Schuyler asked. She smoothed a stack of checklists.

Each dish would be given points out of ten for all the criteria we'd come up with.

I nodded, and my mother called in the first candidate, a business-like Korean American, sent by Miss Lulu.

Her fusion-inspired starters were arranged in flower-shaped bowls, and the jury members sampled everything twice.

Next up was a sinewy guy with heavily tattooed arms and a fondness for ribs and a fiery barbecue sauce. He advertised his business on his butcher's apron as *Adam's Ribs*. "Come on, buddy, have another bite," he said to Steve. "And for the ladies, I've got this. Some of your townsfolk travel 30 miles to get a taste." He uncovered a bowl with a fruity sauce.

The ladies took a tiny portion, but I didn't quite get the impression that they'd hit the road for more of his cuisine.

Adam and his ribs were asked to wait outside, with the others.

Tammy took his place.

"I'm going to sit this one out," Steve said. He marched out of the tent, without so much as a single glance at the woman.

I noticed her ringless finger. It seemed the engagement was off, for better or worse.

Tammy glared daggers at his retreating back until she pulled herself together. "I've prepared a little something I think you'll all enjoy." She snapped her fingers, and Fred rolled in a trolley with two large heat-retaining containers and a basin with creme brulee.

Adriana sniffed the air. So did I.

"Since when have you been cooking?" Primrose asked Tammy. "It seems as if you've been hiding your light under a bushel."

Tammy shuffled her feet. "I only dabbled until recently it was very clear that I'd have to rethink all my life plans. I've done that and now I'm ready for a pivot and the next level." She raised her voice a little. "I don't need a man to help me achieve my dreams."

The Schuylers, both two happy spinsters, broke into encouraging smiles. "Let's see what we can do to support you." Primrose motioned to Fred, who filled a spoonful of a fragrant casserole into four tasting bowls.

Adriana moved closer. "I need a drop to be sure."

"May I? It looks delicious, just like Pierre used to make it." I simpered.

Did Tammy flinch?

"Steve learned from him, and I must have picked up a few things," she muttered.

"Understandably." Aimée dipped her spoon into the bowl and let the food linger in her mouth before she swallowed with obvious enjoyment. "And you've brought dessert, too."

"You should leave that until the end," I said. "You don't want to mix savory and sweet unless you've got a great palate cleanser."

"Yes. Would you be so kind as to wait outside with the others? Only if you don't mind, with Steve being around," my mother said.

Tammy lifted her chin. "No problem at all."

Steve slunk in while the Schuylers and my mother filled in their checklists.

"Poor sap, he's still carrying a torch for that broad," Adriana said.

I'd put my bowl with Tammy's stew on a chair. I held my spoon so that my great-great-aunt could do her version of a lab test.

She was still doing that when Katie entered as the last contender.

She'd dressed for the part in the correct chef's outfit and managed to address all the jurors, while still singling out mom. "I brought you two family recipes," she said. "One stew is with meat, another is a jackfruit dumpling casserole. For dessert, there's a baked Alaska flambé. I've taken the liberty to purchase the ice cream from *Gem and Gelato*." A sly little smile accompanied her explanation.

No doubt she thought she'd earn brownie points with Aimée by using my ice cream.

Fred rolled in another trolley, with Katie's offerings.

Adriana's nostrils flared again as Kate whipped off the covers from her dishes.

"What an interesting combination," Aimée said.

"I think it's so important these days to offer vegetarian and vegan options and to promote them on television." Katie ladled small portions into the bowls and served them up. "I have a list of possible menus if you'd care to see them."

Steve was the only judge not drooling over the food. He shoved his portions aside. "I got a bit of indigestion, sorry."

"Oh, no," Aimée said. "Was it one of the dishes we tried? It's not food poisoning?"

"I'll be fine. No need to fuss."

"Overdose of Tammy," Adriana said.

Silently, I agreed. I secured a bit of both main meals for Adriana and myself.

Like Tammy's, the beef stew was in my opinion a perfect duplicate for Pierre's, only without the final touches. The jackfruit dumplings though did not match his, although they too were familiar enough.

"It's our recipe," Adriana declared after sniffing and tasting the one drop she could eat and sniffing again. "She's the one."

I peeked through the plastic window.

Outside the tent, Jolene strung up twinkling lights, while Officers Newby and Ramos watched.

I hadn't noticed that Tammy had returned, for the battle of the desserts.

Tammy and Katie both arranged their sweets on the worktops.

I'd expected them to show some hostility or at least a bit of tension between each other. I was wrong. Goodwill reigned supreme in the tent, for now.

"That food was quite extraordinary," I said. "Congratulations to both of you."

"Pierre would have been proud to see that the culinary future of Cobblewood Cove is in good hands," Dahlia agreed.

"That's so sweet of you to say," Katie smirked.

"Ins't it?" I said. "Considering you used his exact recipes, the ones his killer stole."

"What?" Tammy's creme brûlée basin crashed to the floor. "Killer? I thought we were going to be partners."

Quick as lightning, Katie grabbed her around the neck and put her in a chokehold. With her other hand she pulled a switchblade knife from her pocket. "Shut up. He and his folks took everything from my family, everything. I gave the man a chance to put things right, but nooo ..." She stopped and scanned her surroundings. She'd switched from polite to manic to cool again at a frightening speed.

The Schuyler sisters stood there, shocked.

Primrose swayed, and Steve hurried to steady her.

Cold sweat trickled down my armpits. I'd hoped to trigger a reaction that would give us real proof. I'd read once that bad people liked to gloat.

That part I got right. Only, I hadn't foreseen all of Katie's actions.

If anything happened to Tammy, it was my fault. Like me, everyone seemed to be holding their breath, as not to trigger her any further.

Steve let go of Primrose. He inched closer.

"Don't move." Karie spat out the words. She bared her teeth in a chilly smirk. "I warn you all, don't try something stupid unless you want Tammy to join Pierre." She used her hostage as a shield as she slowly walked backward.

For an instant, I watched helplessly, without moving a muscle, like the rest of us.

Only Adriana tiptoed to the table with the kitchen tools.

I pointedly stared at one of them, praying silently that Adriana had understood.

"Open the side door," Katie ordered.

She was clever, I had to give her that. The side door meant that the two other candidates sitting in the covered area outside the main entrance wouldn't see her.

Worse still, the police officers might also be unaware of what was going on.

I knelt and pretended to struggle with the heavy zip. The door frame was reinforced with sturdy poles.

"Faster," she said.

Tammy gurgled.

I unzipped the door.

Katie was now only a few inches away from Adriana.

"Now," my great-great-aunt yelled.

A ten-inch-high flame shot out of the blowtorch she'd switched on, next to Katie's ear.

Katie screamed. She dropped the knife and loosened her grip on Tammy.

I pushed the poor woman down and threw the bowl with the hot barbecue sauce into Katie's face.

She howled in pain and covered her eyes.

Steve jumped into the fray. He pinned Katie to the floor while Officers Newby and Ramos came running, with Jolene hot on their heels.

It was over.

Chapter Twenty-Three

"Darling dames, all derring-do, who's the best, well it's those two." Adriana tapped Cleo on the nose. "It was mostly me, but that doesn't rhyme as well."

I let her enjoy her moment of glory. I even wrote down her improvised lyrics. They'd make another entry in the complete works of Adriana Darling, ghostwriter and sleuth.

She sprawled on my bed.

"Do you want to recover here or do you want to come downstairs? There'll be champagne," I said.

She shot up from the bed so fast, that the cat and I both blinked.

"You're not staying like this?" She pointed an accusing finger at my shirt.

"I'm not going to let our friends wait because you'd prefer me to dress up."

"It's up to you if you want to be all spotted and smelling of barbecue sauce."

I peered down at my shirt. 'd overlooked a few tiny splashes on my clothes. "It's evidence of our heroics. Otherwise, I'd need to shower first."

She drummed her fingertips together.

"I'm going down now," I said.

She murmured into Cleo's ear.

I touched Adriana's shoulder, so I'd hear the kitty answer.

"I could lick her and her shirt clean," Cleo offered. "For a prize."

Ungrateful cat. I stalked out of the room.

Adriana overtook me. She curtsied as we entered Aimée's living room, and the assembled crowd broke into applause. "Thank you," she said.

"How did you figure out it was Katie?" Jolene asked. "My cousin says his boss is cheesed off with you, by the way, but he's also super happy their department has closed the case. It'll look great on their performance review."

In the background, I spied Grayson. He had his arm around Daphne's shoulder.

Toto held one paw on his shoe and dozed, so Grayson gave me a sheepish grin. "I can't move right now, otherwise I'd shake your hand," he said.

"I like him," Adriana said. "He's almost good enough for Daphne."

"There were a few things I didn't notice at first," I admitted. "I guess the police found the recipe book in Katie's possession?"

"The book, sleeping pills, and more. Plus there's the confession," Jolene said.

"What things were those?" Tony asked. He and Aimée filled a tray with champagne flutes.

Adriana inhaled. "So many things, ring-a-dings, lotta things."

I'd better hurry up if I wanted her to remember most of this evening, while we had a spellbound audience. "First, there was Pierre, being badgered by her, to take part in that stupid competition. She roped Olivia in as well, in case he'd say yes to Felix's sister."

"Why would she do that, if she wanted to win?" Grayson asked.

"That's what we overlooked. He was to be the man in the background, who handed over his secrets and let her be the face. The same would have happened if he'd partnered with publicity-shy Olivia. When he said no to that, she broke into his office, to steal the book. Afterwards, she had a public argument with him, so he wouldn't suspect her."

"My cousin Hank said she was banging on about how *Butler's Pantry* and the money belonged to her family, because Pierre's granddaddy stole his famous dishes from old Johansson, and her family never saw them again."

"Ridiculous," Aimée said. "If old Butler had done that, all Katie's ancestor needed to do was write them down again."

"That's probably what Pierre told her. He sent her away with a flea in her ear, and she decided he'd blown his chance. Then she poisoned his drink, but she didn't know enough about him to pick the right bottle."

"And then she tried to pin the blame on me," Grayson said.

Toto twitched in his sleep.

Grayson lifted him up. "Do you mind if I sit down with him in my lap?"

"We have a basket here if that's better," Aimée said. She opened a chest and took out Cleo's basket. "I'm afraid it smells like kitty."

"He loves cats," Grayson assured her.

Toto wiggled until Grayson put him down, and the dog climbed into the basket.

Daphne stroked his nose. "I understand why she held a grudge against the Butlers, justified or not. But Sallie had nothing to do with this. Or is Katie at least in this case innocent?"

I shook my head. "She couldn't afford to have people make the connection between her and Pierre's family. As much as she wanted to win those 15 minutes of fame, she needed the police to close the case. So, she gave them suspects who profited from Pierre's death. The fake map we found was a kind of safeguard, in case framing Grayson didn't work out. It was supposed to give the *Carrot Cove* team a much better chance at winning the competition and securing a coveted spot at the fair. When this new suspect then commits suicide, odds are the police wouldn't have looked any further."

"But she couldn't have known that Pierre's booth would go to Felix and the Pottses," Jolene pointed out.

"She didn't have to. I've checked all the minutes. The map we found was only meant to point the investigators toward Sallie. If she'd conveniently died, I'm pretty certain, Pierre's recipe book would have turned up during a search of her belongings."

"Sallie's going to pull through, by the way," Jolene said. "The last news is that she woke up from her coma."

"Thank goodness for that," Aimée said.

"What about Tammy?" Daphne asked.

"Katie was smart. She hedged her bets. First, she found useful partners in Olivia and Felix. She pointed Felix in the direction of Cobblewood Cove once she became aware of her chance at both revenge and promising publicity. Then she drove it home to Olivia that she had to stay in the shadow, for reasons we don't need to go into. At the same time, she worked another angle and became pals with Tammy. All she needed was for Steve to get his hands on the full version of the recipes. Once he'd achieved that, either Tammy would have copied or stolen them, or Katie would have done that. Remember she thought Katie would be her business partner?"

"She would have killed her too," Aimée said.

"It's likely," I said. "But she won't hurt anyone else, and we can all make sure that this fair puts Cobblewood Cove on the map for all the right reasons."

We clinked our glasses.

Adriana hugged the empty bottle. "I want another drink, and I want to dance the Black Bottom. Maybe." She scanned the chandelier and floated off the ground.

I buried my face in my hands. My great-great-aunt was once more inebriated and out of control.

Chapter Twenty-Four

"Delivery coming through," I yelled at the top of my lungs. The borrowed trolley with my ice cream, containers wobbled as I did my best to evade what had to be half of Cobblewood Cove, on the final day of the fair. I should have said no, I thought, as one wheel got stuck and the other three decided to change direction.

Adriana acted as a lookout, sitting atop the trolley.

We'd spent all morning churning and mixing, after a frantic call from the *Cocoa Cabana*.

The last days had been a blur, with police interviews, and arranging the future of *Butler's Pantry* which involved both a takeover, so Grayson could fund his free animal clinic, as well as Steve's continued employment.

Jolene's plans were not quite set in Stone, but we were working on that too.

The trickiest part had been ignoring questions about how the blowtorch had ignited on its own.

A decent amount of sleep would have been nice.

"A little to the left," my great-great-aunt ordered.

"Think of the money," I told myself through gritted teeth as I narrowly avoided a collision with a small boy.

"I think it's fun." Adriana wiggled around.

"Do you need a hand?" a voice behind me asked.

I swiveled around. "Matt!"

"I wish I'd been here sooner," he said. "I've been told you've saved the day yet again."

"Yessir," Adriana said.

"I missed you," Matt murmured.

I used a foot to stop the trolley from rolling away and pulled Matt close. "I missed you too."

"Earth to Genie. You've got a gelato delivery to make." Adriana interrupted what had been a pretty spectacular and very public kiss.

With Matt's help, navigating the final 100 yards was easy.

He carried the containers inside for me, while I stowed away the trolley in the delivery area.

I'd pick it up later and return it to the big tent. For now, the grand finale awaited.

Chefs had cooked, bakers had baked, judges had judged, and Cobblewood Cove waited with bated breath who'd be the winner of the inaugural Silver Spoon and future cover model.

My mother had saved two spots in the front row for me, next to Jilly and her Kenji. My friend's left foot was encased in an orthopedic boot.

Two other seats held place cards for Genie Darling and Genie Darling's guest, from what I could see sticking out from two bottoms firmly planted onto these chairs.

"They're out-of-towners," Aimée mumbled. "Rude, but these seats are better anyway." She rose to greet Matt with two firm pecks on the cheeks.

"Sit down, lady," an impatient voice behind us said.

My mother shot the person a withering glance.

Primrose and Dahlia Schuyler stepped up to the microphone.

Silence fell.

Fred hurried to hand Dahlia a large envelope.

Her sister received a large trophy which she raised into the air. "Ladies and gentlemen, dear friends old and new, it is with the greatest pleasure that we announce the winner of this beautiful trophy and first prize in our culinary competition."

Dahlia took a large card out of the envelope and broke into a delighted smile. "We have two winners. Neely Potts and Olivia Goodge!"

The room erupted into applause.

"What about the photo shoot for the magazine?" Aimée asked me.

"Olivia made it clear that she'd pass up on that option when she entered her name."

Primrose tapped the microphone. "We have one more prize, the Pierre Butler trophy, for best dessert. And the winner is ..."

Her sister stepped up. "Genie Darling, for her homemade artisanal ice cream flavors, *Daredevil's Delight* and *PawPaw's Pleasure**"

"Hooray!" Jilly whistled on her fingers.

The rest of the audience cheered.

Matt nudged me to stand up.

"I don't understand," I said. Nevertheless, I stumbled to the podium where the sisters took turns hugging me.

"Pierre entered you weeks before his death," Primrose said when the noise had stopped. "And the *Cocoa Cabana* let us have all of your ice cream yesterday and today."

"He was very proud of what you created." Dahlia wiped away a tear. "And so should you be."

With the promise to have an engraved cup delivered to me by the end of the week, I returned to my seat.

"We did it." Adriana beamed at me, from my seat. "All is hotsy-totsy again."

And it was, to a certain extent. Outside, people flocked to a stage where a band called *Float Like Candy* proved to be a hit with music lovers of all generations.

Felix had discovered the band at a gig and lured them to Cobblewood Cove.

Matt pulled me into his arms for a dance.

Adriana whirled around us until the band took a break and my feet hurt.

I was almost ridiculously happy, considering the circumstances.

Almost.

There was one item on my to-do list that I'd put off for too long already and I had to change that.

That evening, when Matt, Adriana, and I had wandered home from the fair and stood outside the Darling Villa, I took a deep breath. "I need to tell you something, and I need you to hear me out."

"Am I in trouble?"

"Never." I unlocked the door. "I'll tell you upstairs, and I swear I'm completely sane."

Adriana punched the air. "Finally!"

"All I'm asking is that you listen until I'm finished and ..."

"Genie! Thank goodness you're here." Primrose pressed her hand to her chest until she caught her breath. "It's Petey. He's flown into the chimney flue and won't come out, the poor sweetheart."

Adriana and I both sighed.

"We'll talk later," I said to Matt. "First we've got to rescue a parrot."

Primrose took out a tissue and blew her nose. "We're so grateful to you, Genie. It's like Petey understands every single word you say." Adriana raised both eyebrows.

"It's a gift that's running in the family," I said.

Adriana motioned me to speak on.

"The real pet-whisperer was my great-great-aunt Adriana. Animals adored her." My great-great-aunt fluffed her hair. "They do."

"She was also known for her beauty and her wit."

A little shimmy rewarded me. "Go on."

I fluttered my lashes at Adriana as we climbed into the Schuyler's butler-driven car, to come to Petey's assistance. "Most of all though, she was said to be incredibly modest."

"You must wish you could meet her in person, as an animal lover yourself," Primrose said.

I decided to try a little honesty. "I already feel like I'm incredibly close to her."

"Of course you do." Adriana touched the brick in my purse. Her eyes sparkled, as she recharged. "Inseparable, that's what we are. Now, tell the driver to get a wiggle on. Petey's waiting for our help."

***

A note from Carmen Radtke:

I hope you enjoyed Ghost Stirs The Pot. If you did, please consider leaving a review or a rating on Amazon and BookBub. It makes a huge difference for a book!

Genie and Adriana will return . . .

If you haven't read the first two books in the series, start with Genie and the Ghost and continue with Ghost Takes A Vacation.

If you love Adriana and more conventional golden age mysteries, you'll love the Jack and Frances series, starting with A Matter of Love and Death.

A good girl with a penchant for the truth. A charming law-breaker with a moral code. A retired Vaudevillian who has all kinds of tricks up his sleeve. When it comes to solving crime, these three won't be upstaged by anyone!

About the Author

Carmen has spent most of her life with ink on her fingers, cozy crime plots on her mind (thank you, Agatha Christie) and a dangerously high pile of books and newspapers by her side.

She has worked as a newspaper reporter on two continents and always dreamt of becoming a novelist and screenwriter.

When she found herself crouched under her dining table, typing away on a novel between two earthquakes in Christchurch, New Zealand, she realised she was hooked for life.

The shaken but stirring novel made it to the longlist of the Mslexia competition, and her next book and first mystery, The Case Of The Missing Bride, was a finalist in the Malice Domestic competition in a year without a winner. Since then she has penned several more cozy mysteries, including the Jack and Frances series set in the 1930s.

Ghost Takes A Vacation is the second in a series of fun-filled paranormal cozy mysteries.

In real life, Carmen is absolutely law-abiding, has never met a ghost or been able to communicate with pets (sad, but true). The only time she shed blood and swatted a fly was by accident.

Her wanderlust has led her to live in Germany, New Zealand, and the UK. She currently lives in Italy with her human and her four-legged family.

If you want to keep in touch with her and find out more about her work, writing life, and other related things, sign up for her newsletter on her website www.carmen-radtke.com and receive a free quick read!

Also By

The Genie and Adriana Darling cozy paranormal mysteries
Genie and the Ghost
Ghost Takes A Vacation
Ghost Stirs The Pot

The Jack and Frances cozy 1930s mysteries
A Matter of Love and Death
Murder at the Races
Murder Makes Waves
Death Under Palm Trees
The Mystery of the Christmas Bauble (a novelette)
The Case of the Christmas Angel (a novella)

The Alyssa Chalmers Victorian mysteries

The Case of the Missing Bride
The Prospect of Death
The Tunnels of Doom (coming in 2024)

The cozy contemporary Eve Holdsworth mysteries
Let Sleeping Murder Lie
A Dash of Deceit
Death at the Dog Show
Murder on the Airwaves

Stand-alone novels
Dig Your Own Grave
Walking in the Shadow

Cast of characters

The family

Genie Darling, quick-witted jewelry designer and gelato maker who's in for the surprise of her life

Adriana Darling, Genie's great-great-aunt, a vivacious flapper, who's making the most of her new lease of life as a ghost

Aimée Darling Hepner, Genie's Francophile mother, sadly oblivious to Adriana's presence

Tony Hepner, Aimée's new husband

Cleo, their tabby cat who's under Adriana's spell

The town people

Primrose and Dahlia Schuyler, a couple of mature sisters who run the local museum and most other things in Cobblewood Cove

Pierre Butler, owner of *Butler's Pantry*

Grayson Butler, his nephew, a veterinarian

Steve Hiller, Pierre's chef

Tammy Lee, Steve's ambitious and expensive fiancée

Felicity Goodge, co-owner of rival establishment *Food-stock*

Katie Johnson, Felicity's business partner

Felix Goodge, Felicity's brother and owner of *Vine and Vinyl*

Neely and Sallie Potts, mother and daughter duo and owner of the vegetarian café *Carrot Cove*

Fred Ward, who fills his retirement with volunteer jobs at the library and the museum

Daphne Mills, head librarian

Jolene Ortega, unflappable woman of all trades

Matthew Blake, her second cousin twice removed, art and museum security expert and Genie's boyfriend

Miss Lola, hairdresser and fountain of gossip

Police officer Hank Newby, Jolene's other cousin

Police officer Tilda Ramos, his partner on the job

Petey, a parrot

Champ, a dog